"Where in the World Are You," by Arnold Cross. ISBN 978-1-63868-031-4 (softcover).

Published 2021 by Virtualbookworm.com Publishing Inc., P.O. Box 9949, College Station, TX , 77842, US.

WHERE IN THE WORLD ARE YOU?

CONTENTS

GET TO THE DOCTOR 1

HOW IT ALL STARTED 4

THEY GO TO CANADA 9

WORLD WAR II BREAKS OUT 12

PLANNING A PRISON BREAK 16

JUNE IS ASKING QUESTIONS 17

A PRISON BREAK MAY NOT BE NECESSARY 19

MCCLOUD AT WALTER REED HOSPITAL 22

LET'S SEE WHAT JUNE IS UP TO 26

TIME TO DISCUSS AND ASSESS THE DAMAGE
DONE TO CAPTAIN McCLOUD'S FACE AND LEFT
HAND 28

HERE COMES ANOTHER DOCTOR 30

LET'S CHECK BACK WITH JUNE AND SEE IF SHE
HAS ANY NEWS ABOUT HOLSTONE 35

THE MYSTERY MAN, MR HENDERSON 38

MONDAY MORNING ROLLED IN 41

JUNE IS STILL WORKING ON FINDING HOLSTONE
.... 44

JUNE IS THINKING ABOUT STALKING
HENDERSON 46

JAMES CODY, FROM THE GERMAN PRISON CAMP, IS COMING TO SEE LESTER.................. 50

MR. HENDERSON WAS WAITING FOR JUNE......... 53

LESTER WILL SOON BE DISCHARGED FROM THE HOSPITAL 56

JUNE IS THINKING ABOUT A BETTER PAYING JOB 64

JUNE RETURNS TO HER JOB 72

McCLOUD DECIDES TO TAKE THE JOB AS SQUADRON COMMANDER.......................... 74

MAJOR McCLOUD'S THIRTY-DAY LEAVE IS UP BEFORE HE REALIZES IT 76

MAJOR McCLOUD GETS AN UPGRADE 85

THE MISSION IS ON WITH NEW FASTER PLANES 88

OFF ON TIME AND McCLOUD IS HEADED FOR TROUBLE.................................... 89

BETTER FIND OUT WHAT JUNE IS UP TO 91

THE COLONEL AND LIEUTENANT IN TROUBLE . 97

THE FARMER MUST HAVE TOLD ON THEM 99

MILDRED TAKES THE DETECTIVE OFF THE CASE 104

JUNE HASN'T GIVEN UP NOT BY A LONG SHOT106

WHERE IN THE WORLD ARE YOU? 107

THE GERMANS HAD BEEN WATCHING THE YOUNG BOYS' CAMP................................ 113

CAPTAIN ALBRIGHT TAKES UP THE SLACK 117

THE ROYAL CANADIAN AIR FORCE JOINS FORCES WITH THE AMERICANS AFTER THEIR BASE IS DESTROYED.................................. 120

GATHERING OF THE GENERALS.......................... 122

LESTER AND DONALD ARE STILL MISSING 125

CHANGING THE WAY THE MISSIONS ARE SCHEDULED... 126

THE PILOTS WERE PLEASED FOR THE CHANCE TO SLEEP A LITTLE LONGER 128

GENERAL FLATT RETURNS WITH GOOD NEWS 131

IT APPEARS THE GERMAN SPIES WERE DOING THEIR JOB WELL 132

THE TWO PILOTS THAT WERE SHOT DOWN DID BAIL OUT 134

HITTING CLOSE TO HOME 139

LESTER GOES HOME 141

LESTER TELLS DONALD WHO HE IS 147

LESTER TELLS HIS FAMILY WHO HE IS 149

OH MY GOODNESS 152

GET TO THE DOCTOR

"I DO DECLARE THAT YOUNG MAN WOULD HAVE DIED from the loss of blood if he hadn't made it to our house in time. We realized that Holstone was ready to collapse and rushed him to Dr. Holt. The doctor evaluated the situation and decided that he needed to take him to the hospital where he could get proper care, more care than he could give him. We're his cousins Louise and Morris Sharp"

Since Dr. Holt had heard most of the story on why the boy was brought to him in this condition, he knew very well that it was his duty to report this to the local sheriff. But this would take valuable time, which they didn't have. The boy had lost a lot of blood and time was being wasted. Dr. Holt also knew that it would be a slap on the wrist for the dad and more trouble for the boy if he got the sheriff involved.

On that note he decided to take matters in his own hands and chance anyone finding out how he handled this situation. Besides, this boy was almost like a son to him. Dr. Holt knew he was wasting valuable time and should be on the way to the hospital with this boy, Holstone Mansfield.

Holstone was a young boy twelve years old weighing about seventy pounds. With blond hair and blue eyes, he was a very nice-looking kid until his stepdad got hold of him and messed him up and warped his mind to the point that he couldn't think straight. Sometimes he wasn't sure who he was or where he was. He was lucky to have a friend like Dr. Holt to look after him.

On the way to the hospital Dr. Holt was wondering just how he was going to handle the situation when they got there.

He knew Mr. Wonderland would be looking for the boy and would no doubt come to his office to see if Dr. Holt had seen or treated his stepson or knew the whereabouts of Holstone. Dr Holt was the only doctor in the neighborhood. He had treated the Wonderland family ever since he had come there. He knew he would have to either tell the truth about the boy if Mr. Wonderland came by or sidestep the question to make it sound like he answered it but not really tell a lie.

Dr. Holt knew that Mr. Wonderland had a bad temper. When he got mad about something he lost all control of his emotions, and you couldn't tell him anything. Without a doubt when Holstone was released from the hospital and went back home the trouble would start again.

So, Dr. Holt decided to admit Holstone under an assumed name to keep Mr. Wonderland from finding him. He also knew that he could get into real trouble if the truth was ever found out. He could lose his license to practice medicine, but he knew that Holstone's life was in danger, and he was the only one that could give him the help he needed.

Dr. Holt was a man about fifty years old with blond hair and blue eyes. He was well known and liked in the neighborhood. He was also the only doctor for several miles around so he treated people for whatever the ailment might be jack of all ailments you might say. Of course, that's what country doctors do. He was married to a wonderful woman, Amanda. She and Dr. Holt had two children, Frank, was the oldest at 14 and, Shirley, was three years younger

Dr. Holt didn't tell his wife Amanda about the young boy and what he did that might cause him a lot of trouble if the wrong person found out about what he had done for the boy. Plus, it would just cause his wife to worry. So, he would do the worrying. Also, she might just say the wrong thing to the wrong person not thinking just what it could do to them. So, on that note he would just go it alone. The fewer people who knew about what he was doing the better. Dr. Holt wasn't a man to get involved in things like this every day but in this case the boy Holstone meant a lot to him. In fact, Dr. Holt had brought Holstone into this world and doctored him up through life as he did the whole family, so he felt something special about this young lad and he was willing to stick his neck out a bit for him.

HOW IT ALL STARTED

THE TROUBLE STARTED WHEN THE KIDS were all out playing. One of Holstone's sisters Hester told him that she was going to tell their father that he was picking on her and pushed her off the porch and was throwing dirt in her eyes and that he had been doing this sort of thing for a long time.

Holstone said, "You know that isn't true. You're always telling things that are not true and causing trouble in our family. Why can't you be like the rest of the family and get along with your brother and sisters?"

Hester said, "I'm going to tell Father anyway and let him give you the good thrashing you deserve. He gets pretty mean when he's been drinking."

Holstone went on repairing his fishing gear, not thinking any more about what his sister had said to him. He was so engrossed in his work he didn't hear his father walk up behind him, but he did get a whiff of whatever his father had been drinking.

His father asked, "Holstone, why did you do that to your sister?"

Holstone said, "Father, I didn't do anything to her. She is lying as always and trying to cause trouble in the family."

His stepfather grabbed him and took him to the house, got a straight back chair, pushed him down on it, and tied him to it. He also tied the boy's hands behind his back. He got a horse whip and started whipping on Holstone until the boy was almost ready to pass out. Then he headed to the barn.

Holstone didn't know why his stepfather was going to the barn, but he knew it was for something to do more harm to him and was, for sure, no good. He kicked off his bloody slacks and shoes. That only left him with a long shirt tail to cover some of his vital parts which had been damaged by the whipping.

Dark was moving in fast, and Holston knew this was his chance to get away. It was now or never. He started running as best he could. Needless to say, running was almost impossible, but he knew time was running out for him. He made it to the railroad tracks, although the rocks were taking their toll on his feet.

Holstone made it to his cousin's house with the chair still tied to him and his hands tied behind his back. He backed up to the door and banged on it with the chair.

His cousin opened the door and when she saw Holstone standing there with blood dripping off what was left of his clothes she said, "My God, what has happened to you?"

She called her husband, Morris Sharp, and said, "We had better get Holstone to the doctor."

Morris said, "Louise it's late. I hope Dr. Holt's home. All we can do is hope and get there as soon as we can."

On the way to the doctor Holstone told them the story leaving out nothing. Before they left the house Louise tried to tie some clothing around where the blood was coming from, but it didn't help. Holstone was still bleeding, and it ruined the seat of the car.

Holstone said, "I'm terribly sorry I've ruined the seat. I don't have any way of paying you for what you're doing for me or for ruining your car seat. But someday I'll have money and I'll pay you for all this."

Dr. Holt was home. Morris and Louise told him what they knew about Holstone as Dr. Holt checked him over. This only took a few minutes.

Then Dr. Holt said, "We're on our way to the hospital. Keep this under your hat please."

Dr. Holt wasn't sure if Holstone was alert enough to understand what he needed to know. But he was going to tell him anyhow and hope for the best, because it needed to be discussed between them and now. Dr. Holt asked Holstone if he was awake enough to understand what he was saying to him.

Holstone said "Yes, the pain pills that you gave me are working. They make me feel a lot better."

Dr. Holt asked Holstone if he was going back home after he was released from the hospital.

Holstone said, "No, but on the other hand I really don't know what to do. I have no money. I'm not old enough to get a job. It looks like I'm stuck. If I could get some clothes, I guess I could go to another town.

"But to do that I'd need clothes and enough money to at least buy food until I got work and a payday, little money to keep myself halfway spruced up. I've got a few dollars at home that I've saved but I don't dare go back to get it and there' no one in the family I would trust to bring it to me and keep it quiet. But if I went to another town I'd have to lie about my age, and get work, at least make enough money to live on. But Dr. Holt, sir, I don't know how I'm going to pay this hospital bill and you for taking care of me."

Dr. Holt said, "Don't you worry about those things. I'm taking care of the bills and I'll have some new clothes here when you are ready to be discharged."

Holstone said, "How will I ever be able to repay you and thank you for what you are doing for me?"

Dr. Holt said, "Let me run this by you and see what you think about it. I've been doing some thinking and I think I've got a plan for you that will work. It's a dangerous thing to be messing with but I realize that if you go home the trouble with you and your stepfather will start again. It could be death for you the next go around.

"This plan I've been thinking about, should you go for it, could cause me a lot of trouble, maybe even prison time. It must be kept under your hat at all costs. I have some longtime friends in Canada. They have no kids and I think they would love to have a son like you. If you think you would possibly like to do this, I'll give them a call and see what they think about it."

At first, Holstone didn't think much about leaving the country but on the other hand, he didn't have another choice.

He said to Dr. Holt, "If you think this is the best thing for me, I'll go, that is if your friends will take me."

Dr. Holt said, "I'll have the news for you one way or the other on my next visit with you." He said, "One more thing, do you think your cousins will keep this thing quiet?"

Holstone said, "I'd bet my life on it."

Dr. Holt said, "That's good news."

Holstone was checked into the hospital as planned, under an assumed name. For the time being he would have the name of Cantrell Wagner. After they got to Canada the McClouds would give him a first name.

The McClouds, who lived in Canada, were longtime friends of Dr. Holt and were the family that Wagner would be adopted into, that is if he didn't chicken out on the deal that Dr. Holt was setting up for him. Of course, he probably would not chicken out simply because he didn't have any other choice. If he went back to his family his stepdad would always give him trouble. He could do severe damage to the young man, even kill him. This is the best deal he could possibly ever get.

Before he left the hospital, Dr. Holt said one more thing, "If this set up goes through you will get a new name and no one will ever know where you were born or who you were before."

Dr. Holt went back to the hospital two days later as promised. Dr. Haynes, Wagner's doctor at the hospital, told Dr. Holt that when he gave Wagner a good going over, he found more damage to the boy's body than he had expected. There was quite a bit of damage to parts of Wagner's body, and he was running a fever.

"On that note," Dr. Haynes said, "I'm going to keep him another two days and see if the infection clears up."

Dr. Holt said, "Fine by me. I need to do some thinking."

As soon as Wagner's room cleared of people, Dr. Holt said, "I hope you are ready for this. I spoke with my friends John and Betty McCloud in Canada last night. They are delighted about the possibility of having a son. As I told you, they don't have any children.

"I think this will be a great move for you. It's for sure you don't have a chance here and don't have any other road to travel. I'll call John and Betty and we'll drive up to their home in Canada if you still want to go through with this deal.

"I'm sure you have been in deep thought about going out of the country to live and maybe never being able to come back here, especially for a great long time. I'll admit it is a big step and it deserves a heap of thinking."

Wagner said, "I'm ready."

Dr. Holt said, "I've been wanting to see them anyway. I told Dr. Haynes that we're going on a little trip as soon as you were able. But I didn't tell him where."

Dr. Holt called a friend and asked him to see his patients for him for the next week.

When Wagner was released from the hospital, Dr. Holt took him to a clothing store and bought several outfits for him from the floor up both winter and summer.

THEY GO TO CANADA

DR. HOLT SAID, "LET'S HEAD FOR CANADA."

This was a long trip for a boy who had just gotten out of the hospital. They stopped and took a fifteen-minute break every two or three hours. Dr. Holt asked Wagner if he was feeling ok. Finally, they arrived in Edmonton, Canada.

Dr. Holt said, "Let's stop and have a meal, something light, more like a snack, because the McClouds want to take us out for dinner tonight, which isn't too long from now. Anyway, we'll freshen up a bit before we get to your new parents' house."

The McClouds were very pleased to see Dr. Holt and their new son.

John McClould said, "I've got the perfect restaurant picked out for us tonight for this special occasion. I hope that's agreeable with everyone."

They went to one of the best restaurants in town. Wagner couldn't say a word. Seeing all that beauty, he thought he was dreaming. The food was as great as the place was beautiful. When they got back to the McClouds' home, everybody wanted to talk, they had so much to talk about. It had been a long time between visits with the McClouds and Dr. Holt. No one mentioned the problem between Wagner and his stepfather and that suited Wagner just fine. After a few drinks and a lot of talk someone mentioned that it had been a long day. Dr. Holt and Wagner were shown to their rooms.

John said, "See you at breakfast at seven o'clock."

Dr. Holt and Wagner were worn out from the trip, so they didn't waste any time getting to sleep. Before they realized it, it was time to get up.

Mr. McClould was calling out, "Breakfast in ten minutes." The McClouds had the day planned out, showing Dr. Holt and Wagner where he, Wagner, would be attending school and where Mr. McCloud was principal, the market where they shopped for groceries, the post office, hospital, and several other things. They had lunch around noon. Finally, it was time to go home again.

After three days, Dr. Holt was ready to head back to his home and office, He said goodbye to all and went on his way. After dinner that night the McClouds took Wagner to the sitting room and began to lay out the way life was going to be for him.

"You will be required to go to school, then college. You will get a new name for security purposes," John said. "We have selected several first names and middle names for you. This is the list that I've written out. Look them over and select one that you like. I know you must be getting tired and confused with all these name changes, but it's all for the best if we want to make the plan work that Dr. Holt came up with. As he told you, be careful who you talk to at school, or any time and what you say to them. Since you are an American, they will be wondering what you are doing here and be asking questions. I am the principal at the school. But talk could cause us all much trouble."

Wagner looked over the list and asked, "Would you call me Lester?"

When Louise and John got Lester settled in his room, they went to their bedroom.

John said to Louise, "Dear, we may have just done one of the stupidest things in history. If Lester's family ever learns of this, we could be in real trouble, along with Dr. Holt.

"Now, since I'm the principal of the school I could come up with an iron clad alibi on why a young American boy is in our school. I suppose we should take care of the adoption papers right away.

"I've said it many times that one lie always creates another to cover the first one. But I guess one more won't hurt any more than the first one. We'll just play it that way and hope for the best.

"We'll cut back on our visiting with folks and cut down on our invitations to friends. We'll just tell them that we are getting a bit older each year.

"We can start going out more since Lester will be with us after school. We can go to out to eat more and there are always movies and so much more that I'm sure Lester hasn't seen. It will all work out."

Lester got along well with his new parents. They were very pleased with him.

After he finished college, Lester started working on a degree in medicine, which pleased Louise and John more than they could say. Also, Lester wanted to do this for the man who had done so much for him, Dr. Holt.

WORLD WAR II BREAKS OUT

HOWEVER, WORLD WAR II BROKE OUT and the Canadian government was sending troops, aircraft, pilots as well as many other materials to aid the English and the Americans. Lester was drafted and wound up in flying school. He was commissioned and became a fighter pilot.

After his flight training, he was stationed in England where the Canadian fliers worked with the British and the American Air Force. Lester felt kind of odd since he was a real American working with the American Air Force as a Canadian, but he had to keep quiet about who he really was. Sometimes he really wanted to yell out "I'm a Yank" as the British call the Americans, but his thoughts went back to the beginning of his misery. So, he clammed up on that note and said to himself, "I'm a Royal Air Force officer from Canada."

Since he had gone to school in Canada, he picked up the accent, so everybody thought he was a real Canadian. He did dream of home quite a bit, that is the home when he was a kid. Of course, he realized that he couldn't ask for a better home and more loving parents than the McClouds. They educated him and taught him to be a gentleman and put him where he was today.

When he was flying at times his mind wanted to ramble off to dream about something that happened at home when he was a kid. But he brushed it off for the time being because dreaming about something like that while you are flying, especially in enemy country, can get you killed so he kept his mind on what he was doing and where he was. But sometimes Lester couldn't believe that he had advanced to an officer in the

Royal Air Force especially since he came from the hills of Tennessee without a dime in his jeans.

Never a day went by that he didn't thank God for giving him a special friend like Dr. Holt and parents like the McClouds. How lucky can a person get? Of course, sometimes he didn't think there was such a thing as luck. It was just meant to be like that - it was the work of God.

After about ten or twelve missions over Germany, he was shot down.

He was stuck in the aircraft wreckage for about twelve hours. During that time, he thought of several things he should have done but didn't. The weather was cold. It started to snow. Lester wondered if he was going to freeze to death before someone found him.

Around midnight an animal that looked like a wolf came to visit him. It just kept circling the wreckage and Lester knew that it was feeling things out, maybe waiting for some help from a friend. The animal could smell Lester's blood. It knew the man was helpless. It was just a matter of time before he pounced on the man.

Lester had a side arm but the way he was pinned in the wreckage he wasn't able to get his hand on it. He was left-handed. He didn't know if he could handle the weapon with his right hand even if he could get his hand on it. Pinned in the wreckage like he was he didn't think he could hit the animal using his right hand but all he could do was wait and see and give it his best shot if it became necessary. He was tired and began to dose off. He noticed the animal was aware of that and moved in a bit closer.

That got Lester's attention. He started working a bit harder trying to get the weapon which was pinned under him. He finally got his fingers on the weapon just enough to pull it out from underneath him. By that time the animal was really getting close, and Lester was frightened. By that time, he had the weapon in his right hand. He said to himself, "Here goes"

13

and fired. He missed but the animal got the message. tucked his trail and left the scene.

Now Lester started worrying about if anyone would find him, and was anyone looking for him? A little after daybreak he heard someone talking and it wasn't English.

The Germans had to cut away some of the aircraft fuselage to get him out of the aircraft. He understood one of the two men to say, "Ah let's just leave him in there, he's no good to us in the shape he's in. We'll just have to feed him and spend money on him for medicine and get no work from him."

The other soldier said, "We'll cut him out. He may give up some useful information. After all, he is just a kid."

He was taken to the prison camp, but he was in such bad shape from the crash that he stayed in the hospital most of the time. He needed some reconstruction done on his face and on his left hand. It was crushed very badly from the crash. The doctor in the prison camp didn't do any more for the prisoners than just enough to keep them alive.

Before they put him in a hospital, if you could call it a hospital, he was locked in what they called a cell for three days, no bed just straw on the floor and very little food. After they put him in what they called a hospital the food was a little better but nothing to brag about. A person sure wouldn't get fat eating it. The doctor came by every two days but didn't do much except look at his wounds and say something that Lester couldn't understand.

Then here came the interrogation team wanting to know all sorts of things that Lester didn't know beans about. One of the men did speak English and he told Lester that they could torture him to the point to where he would think that he was going to die. They believed that would persuade him to talk and tell them what they wanted to know. If he died in the process, it didn't matter to them because there was nothing lost. He kept telling them that he was just an aircraft pilot and didn't know anything about what they were asking.

The English speaking one said, "We will see how he does without food or water for about three days and then I think he will be glad to talk for a plate of food and a big glass of water." As it turned out those three days never came.

PLANNING A PRISON BREAK

LIEUTENANT MCCLOUD GOT TO KNOW ANOTHER PRISONER James Cody very well while they were both in the prison hospital. They started planning to break out just as soon as they were well enough to run, unless they got a chance to commandeer a vehicle for the getaway. It was, of course, very unlikely for them to get their hands on any type of transportation with wheels, but a soldier tries everything and anything to get out of an enemy prison camp. Cody was an American and an expert at picking locks.

He said to Lester, "I haven't found a lock yet that I can't pick. After the doctor leaves tonight, I'll take a look around, maybe pick a lock or two and see what I can find out. I'll take a look at the distance to the gate and what's beyond. Maybe see if there are any vehicles parked close by overnight.

"I'll see what I can find out about the night guards, where they are, how many, and where their barracks are, things like that. Guards tend to let their guard down at night after the supervisors have gone home. Some of them play around all day or have a day job. When night comes, and the supervisors leave for the day then the night guard will get his sleep. I'll be back soon and fill you in on what I find out. If we do have a chance to escape, when our health gets a little better, we'll go for it. But we don't want to rush this thing and get your face wounds infected any more than they already are."

JUNE IS ASKING QUESTIONS

JUNE, LESTER'S (HOLSTONE'S) HALF-SISTER was born after he disappeared. She started asking her family questions about him. The answers were always the same. Her mother, Alice, just told her that she looked out the kitchen window just in time to see her husband tie Holstone to a chair. He used a horse whip on him. By the time she got outside the whipping had stopped.

She went on, "I had things cooking on the stove. When I finished tending to that and went outside. Holstone was gone. I thought he had just stepped behind the woodshed, but I later learned that he was gone, and no one could find him on the property.

"The day turned dark. A storm was moving our way. Your father came in the house and got a carbide light. I later learned that he went down the railroad tracking Holstone by his blood drops until the storm moved in and he lost the tracks.

"He returned an hour later wet to the skin. He went to his room without his supper. From that I knew he was upset with himself. Of course, he's a man who never says much anyway.

"It rained most of the night. The creek and rivers were out of their banks by morning. When we saw that, we figured the worst for Holstone. That's all that any of us know."

June said, "I'm going to try something, and I'll need your help to do it. I'm going to act like Holstone running down the railroad with a chair tied to his back and his hands tied behind his back and see how far I get before the rainstorm hits. I'll run until I get tired and see where I wind up. If it's close to a house I'll ask questions, that is if they were living there during that time. It's worth a try. I've always said that if you don't try then you will never know."

Her mother said, "Good luck and don't get run down by a coal train."

A PRISON BREAK MAY NOT BE NECESSARY

A PLAN WAS IN THE WORKS in the intelligence section to overrun the prison camp that coming Sunday night. The Americans, working with the British and Canadians, had come up with what they thought was a fail-safe plan to invade the prison and bring the prisoners out safely. They agreed that Sunday night was good since it was a German holiday. People tend to get lax on a weekend and especially at night.

Lester and his friend, James, didn't know anything about this plan, so they were working on their own plan of escape. Of course, that would be a little ways away since they were both in pretty bad shape, McCloud with infected face lacerations, and Cody with severe burns from a gasoline fire. His truck was overturned when an enemy bomb exploded.

The crew on a reconnaissance plane had mapped and taken photos of the prison camp. The rescue crew knew pretty well where every building was and what was in it. They figured since it was a German holiday and a Sunday night that the officer in charge wouldn't be on duty there. Just before midnight on Sunday the rescue crews were set to go and overrun the prison camp.

A river ran along the entire back of the prison. It had rained heavily for the past week and the river was out of its banks. The rushing water made a lot of noise and made good cover for the helicopter's noise. Since there were an estimated 150 prisoners in the camp, the rescue team needed quite a few pieces of equipment to get the prisoners out safely. The Canadians had several big helicopters, Sikorsky R-4s.

The commanding officer had set up four waves of rescuers, each team with a helicopter. There were two spare helicopters that would remain hidden unless they were needed. Each team had three - not more than four minutes on the ground for loading the prisoners.

The first wave brought in a swat team of ten men. They were down in the middle of the prison grounds. They had machine guns, flame throwers, grenades and as much explosives as they could carry. The first helicopter made its rounds with a machine gun operator shooting from each side. That gave the swat team on the ground the advantage. This entire affair was set up to take about twelve to fifteen minutes and then be gone. Of course, the team didn't know for sure how many of the prisoners were bedridden. That, in itself, could take up quite a bit of time.

By the time the weapons fire and other explosions ceased, all the German guards, cooks, chiefs and bottle washers were wiped out. The second wave of the rescue team was inside the walls of the prison camp. By then, the first wave was loaded and leaving the scene with a group of prisoners. There was only enough ground space for two helicopters to land.

There were four waves of rescue teams set up for this operation. The allotted time set up for each wave to be on the ground and gone was three minutes. The first helicopter was leaving as the third one was landing. The second one was just about ready to go.

Lt. McCloud was standing by for the third wave. He was looking around, trying to locate James Cody. He asked a person standing by him if he had seen Cody.

The man said, "I know him, but I haven't seen him since this raid started. There is so much confusion and noise going on, it's hard to find out anything.

"However, someone did say that some prisoners got shot and killed in the first raid, as the second helicopter was leaving with its load and the fourth one was landing."

They were running out of time. They had been on the ground over their time limit. The planners had this rescue clocked down to the second, very close to when the townspeople would get word of what was happening.

The German army would be there in no time and all hell would break loose. But the timing, if it went to schedule, would put the rescue teams and prisoners out and several miles away from the prison camp by the time more Germans got there. If they didn't have weapons with them, they would have a hard time finding one that would operate in the mess that the swat teams left the prison.

Number four was the last wave. Since they weren't fully loaded with prisoners they managed to find and load four KIAs (killed in action). They were running out of time. They could hear sirens in the distance. All four helicopters, plus the two spares that weren't needed, made the flight to a safe base in England.

McCloud started searching for his friend, Cody. But no one had seen him, and he wasn't one of the four KIAs. There wasn't anything that could be done now. He couldn't go back to the prison camp. Needless to say, the Germans would be a bit upset with them, but that was just too bad.

Several of the prisoners were in bad health and had to be hospitalized including McCloud.

The ones admitted to the hospital would be evaluated and be sent to the states where they could be treated properly. With the war going on the overseas hospitals could get mighty crowded at times.

McCloud was scheduled to go to Walter Reed hospital, in Washington, D.C. He asked the doctor if he could send him to Edmonton, Canada. The doctor said, "It's not my call. These things are set up by the Army staff. Walter Reed has the better plastic surgeons. From what I see you need the best. Recovery is going to take a long time."

McCloud at Walter Reed Hospital

MCCLOUD ARRIVED at Walter Reed on Friday.

His doctor came and introduced himself. "I'm Dr. Jeff McKinley," he said. "I'll be your doctor until you are well enough to go back to duty."

The doctor examined the lacerations on McCloud's face and hand.

He said, "Jackie, my nurse, will put something on these infected places. I'll see you Monday and we will get started on seeing what we can do."

McCloud asked, "Is there some way to keep the reporters out of my room? The orderly that pushed my wheelchair in here had to practically beat them off with a stick. I don't want my picture taken and I sure don't want it in the newspapers. I just want to be left alone."

Dr. McKinley assured him that he would see to it that the reporters stayed away from him. He left and soon the nurse arrived with all types of medicine to be put on his lacerations. She had brown eyes.

"I'm Jackie Newton. I work with Dr. McKinley. I'll be your nurse as long as you are here. So, for now, I'll put some antibiotic cream on your face to help get rid of the infection and make it a little easier for you. Do you have any pain at this time?"

McCloud said, "I could use a pain pill and some food."

Jackie said, "I'll get the pill and food just as soon as I take care of this. On weekends another nurse will be taking care of you. I'll be your nurse Monday through Friday."

McCloud rested Saturday and Sunday. However, late Sunday night he needed something for the pain in his face. He called the nurse and told her that he needed something for pain. She gave him a pain pill.

Monday morning, he got a big breakfast. He was just finishing eating when a knock on the door got his attention.

His Jackie looked in and said, "Some important Army officers are here to speak with you. May they come in?"

He said, "Just as long as they're not reporters."

She said, "No reporters."

Three Canadian military officers came in the room and introduced themselves as, Colonel Jesse York, Major Phillip Jones, and Captain John Kelly.

Cpt. Kelly said, "State your full name and rank please."

"Lieutenant Lester McCloud, Serial number ------, Canadian Air Force."

"Very good," said the captain, "Now why are you here?"

McCloud said, "I'm a pilot. My plane was shot down over Germany. I was taken prisoner. I was in a prison hospital for eight months. I might add that very little was done to help my condition. A week ago, a team of Americans, English, and Canadians rescued all the prisoners. I was sent here for surgery to my face and left hand."

Col. York said, "Well done Cpt. McCloud."

McCloud said, "Sir, I'm just a lieutenant."

Col. York said, "I have orders here promoting you to Captain. Also, this order is to award you the Canadian Sacrifice Medal."

Captain McCloud said, "Wish I was able to buy you guys a drink."

Col. York said, "Maybe some time later."

He told McCloud, "Your parents have been called and notified of where you are. But that's all they know. They should be here sometime today. If you need anything that we can help with let us know and thank you for your service."

McCloud got into a sad mood after the officers left. He was thinking about his friend from the prison camp. Did he make it out, or was he killed in the raid or shot up and left behind? It's sad to say and think about, but the rescue team had been on a tight schedule. They had no way of knowing all the names of the prisoners, no time to take roll call. So many minutes on the ground in the prison camp and gone.

Then his mind went to his family that he left in such a hurry, with no time to say goodbye. Without a doubt in his mind, they were all wondering, and had been for as long as he had been gone, was he still alive, was he dead or could something else be the problem? What was it that kept him from letting them know he was still alive? He felt guilty for what he was doing to them. He guessed deep down he really wanted to be with them, but he knew that couldn't be. Too much was at stake. He had no other choice but to go on as he was doing.

His thoughts were changed by a light knock on his door.

A man's head came around the door and said, "Are you decent?"

McCloud said, "It's my loving Dad, of course I'm decent."

Mom ran in front of Dad and threw her arms around her son and said, "My god! What happened to your face?" McCloud tried to explain what had happened.

About all he could say was, "Flying broken glass and ripped up metal can do bad things to the skin. Now how are my wonderful parents doing?"

John said, "We are doing fine, now that we know you are back in non-hostile territory, and not in some stinking prison camp in another country. I can tell you've lost weight, so I'm guessing that they didn't feed you very well in prison. But I guess that's part of their game. I'm just well pleased that you are here. I'm sure the Americans will take very good care of you and feed you well. I wish that they could have sent you closer to home, but we want the best for you. I see that you have been awarded the Sacrifice Medal."

Lester said, "And promoted to Captain as of last week."

After McCloud's parents left for home, he had a good night's rest. He was ready to find out just what his doctor was going to do and about how long this ordeal was going to last.

LET'S SEE WHAT JUNE IS UP TO

JUNE'S MOTHER, ALICE WONDERLAND, helped her with the chair and the ropes. Down the road she went. The way she was humped over she looked like a bull getting ready to charge.

As she ran down the road she was thinking, "This isn't getting me anywhere in my investigation. I need to attack it in another way. Of course, I knew when I started this it wasn't going to be a piece of cake. What I need to do is get myself a job at a newspaper. That will give me access to a lot of ways to put out the word. That way it won't cost me so much."

June went to the big city of Overton and applied for a job at the newspaper, The Golden Age. She was called in the next day for an interview. She got the job and went to work as a copy boy. After she told the staff who she was and what she was doing to try to find out something about her half-brother, they were all willing to help her as much as possible. She got to know folks from other towns that worked for newspapers. After hearing her story, they were willing to help her try and find her half-brother Holstone.

Her younger sister Mildred joined her on her quest from time to time, but she had other things to do and really didn't have the time. She did what she could to help.

Her brother Joseph would go with June when she went out of town and needed to stay overnight. He was a lot of help to her.

Joseph asked June, "Do you think you would know Holstone if you passed by him on the street?"

She said, "Good question. It has been a long time and neither one of us has ever seen him. I may very well be wasting my time and yours. And it's costing a lot of money. But I have dreams that he is still alive somewhere. But where? And why he is staying away? It just keeps my mind all mixed up and will make me old and gray before my time. What do you think about what you just asked me?"

Joseph said, "I really doubt if I would recognize him. Sometimes, when you are looking so hard for someone, finally all faces seem to blend into each other, and it's very difficult to sort them out from one another. Wasting your time and mine. I don't know about that. Myself, I try and figure out, that is if he is still alive, what keeps him from trying to get in touch with at least some of us. That part is a mystery to me. This is something that might shock you. He could be walking among us and since we have never seen him, we just might not know him. I don't much think so but most anything is possible. So, let's keep looking and searching all avenues. I'm with you on the search as much as time will allow me.

TIME TO DISCUSS AND ASSESS THE DAMAGE DONE TO CAPTAIN McCLOUD'S FACE AND LEFT HAND

JACKIE NEWTON, MCCLOUD'S NURSE, came in and said, "I'll give you your medication. Your breakfast is on the way, so is your doctor. By the way how was your weekend?"

McCloud said, "Most of it was great. I got orders promoting me to captain and orders awarding me the Sacrifice Medal. Then my parents came to visit me. That made my weekend."

Jackie said, "Your doctor will be in at seven with his staff of surgeons. First, they will assess the damage to your face and left hand. They'll then decide on just what they need to do and what special equipment they will need. Some items will need to be special ordered. If they're not here on time, the game plan will be delayed or even lost, and they will need to start over with some of the things that have already been done. What it boils down to is this - it isn't a simple job that's being planned. But they are all good at what they do. They work in shifts as needed. After each day's work on your lacerations, they will let you rest for at least twelve hours before another round of work. I think you will like them and what they can do."

Dr. McKinley came with his staff of doctors.

He said, "Gentlemen, this is Lieutenant Lester McCloud."

McCloud said, "Dr. McKinley, it's Captain McCloud, and let's drop the captain and call me Lester."

"That it will be," said Dr. McKinley, "The doctors who will be working with me are Dr. Insole Lackland, Robert Church, Irvin Stonehill, and Mike Yearmaster, and, of course, your favorite doctor, Jeff McKinley, at your service. That's quite a line up, don't you think?

"Now this is what we are going to do: initially, we are going to find out what we need to do first and set up a schedule for our work and also your rest time. The stress of all this can sometimes get to the point that it wears you down and your resistance gets low. We don't want that. So, your time off is important too. All this will begin as soon as we get the infection under control So on that note we will get started." The day went well, with the doctor's team discussing what they needed to do the job.

HERE COMES ANOTHER DOCTOR

MCCLOUD'S OLD FRIEND, DR. HOLT, stuck his head in the door and said, "Do you need another doctor by any chance."

McCloud said, "I can always use one like you. So come on in and let me hug your neck and shake your hand. I know I must be a sight to look at but seeing you takes all those thoughts away with the pain, at least for the time being. A lot has happened since I last saw you. So much that I really don't know where to start. Sometimes it all seems like just a dream, then I pick up a mirror and the face that's looking back at me tells me that I'm not dreaming, that its real - hell, and reality.

"The Germans got me while I was flying over them. I was imprisoned after they shot me down. I was rescued from the camp by the Americans, English and Canadians. The lacerations to my face and left hand got infected because the doctors in the camp gave me very little medical care or none at all. But God has been with me and I'm here in good hands and alive.

"Now, Dr. Holt, how have you been?"

"I'm doing just fine," Dr. Holt said, "Business has been good. Your stepfather has been to visit me twice in the past few years. He always mentions you. I don't think he suspects anything, at least he doesn't let on. Your half-sister June who was born after you left has been asking me a lot of questions about you and other things that I can't answer."

McCloud wanted to know what she looked like. Dr. Holt said, "I have a picture of her that I got just for you. Can't tell when you may want to know what she looks like. There is another half-sister and two half-brothers who were born after you left. Your other half-sister's name is Mildred, two half-brothers are Joseph and Harm. The way June talked to me about you I don't think she will give up on looking for you unless she finds some concrete evidence that you're dead. We know that isn't going to happen. I understand that she has landed a job with a newspaper in Overton, so she might reach out pretty far, looking for you."

McCloud said, "The way my face looks right now I doubt that anyone would recognize me as who I was as a youngster. I'm thinking that I'm going to look quite different after the surgery. I've asked Dr. McKinley to keep the reporters out of my room. I don't want any pictures taken of me, so that's taken care of. So, I guess I'll just have to wait and see what I look like when the surgery is finished."

Dr. Holt asked what time McKinley had given for finishing the surgery.

McCloud said, "They didn't really give me a finish date, but did mention that it would most likely be close to a year."

McCloud thought this would be as good a time as any to let Dr. Holt know that he was interested in keeping up his study of medicine. He thought since he was sure to be there a year, that he may as well get back to his study of medicine while he was in the hospital. He could accomplish quite a bit while the doctors worked on him, especially since Dr. McKinley told him that this would be more or less twelve hours of work on McCloud and twelve hours of rest. He could get a lot of studying done in twelve hours.

Dr. Holt said, "Let me know if I can help. I'm pleased you're following in my footsteps. That is certainly an honor. I must tell you it's been wonderful to visit with you. I'll admit it is sad for me to see you all bandaged up like that. I just hope the operations work out for you. I'm leaving now but since you will be here for some time, I'll be back."

McCloud had a good night's rest after Dr. Holt left. He was happy with his visit with his old friend. It gave him a lift. The next day was Tuesday. He got on the phone early, checking on how he could get the information he needed to continue his study of medicine.

His nurse, Jackie, came in with his daily morning medicine and told him his breakfast was on the way. She also told him who to call to get the information he needed to continue his studies.

McCloud also made a couple of calls asking about his friend from the German prison, Sgt. James Cody. After several more calls he learned from the sergeant in charge of the rescue team that Sgt. Cody made an escape on foot just before the gun fire started. He was picked up a few days later by the rescue team. He was dehydrated and weak from the lack of food and water, but all in all, he was ok.

Lester asked the sergeant if he knew where Sgt. Cody was stationed.

The sergeant said, "I think he is stationed at Wright Paterson Air Force Base, Ohio."

McCloud called the base locater and sure enough they found him. Cody called McCloud right away. They had a long talk.

Cody said, "I'll be down to visit with you in the next few days."

McCloud got to know one of his orderlies rather well. Bill Raye, the orderly, realized, that McCloud would get bored on the weekends since he couldn't get out on his own. So, he asked McCloud if he would like to go home with him for the weekend. McCloud jumped at the offer.

Bill said, "My wife and I live quite a way out in the country. It's quiet. There is a good-sized lake on the property for fishing. We could fish from the pier or a small wooden boat."

McCloud said, "I'd love to go."

"I must ask Dr. McKinley," Bill said, "If it's ok to take you out of the hospital for a weekend."

When Bill asked Dr. McKinley if it were ok to take McCloud home with him for the weekend, Dr. McKinley said, "Sure, it will do him good to be out for a few hours."

Friday, after his shift, Bill loaded McCloud into his station wagon and headed home. Saturday morning, they all went sight-seeing.

Bill's wife, Kathie said, "Lester might like to see the downtown fish market and the beach. He wouldn't have to get out of the car unless he wanted to so he can see all these things. You can see a lot from the car."

Bill said, "It's time for lunch. What would you like for lunch Lester?"

Lester said, "If it's up to me I'd say sea food."

Bill asked Kathie if sea food was ok with her. It was.

Bill said, "Sea food it is."

After lunch Bill said, "We don't want to wear Lester out on his first day out. So, I guess we'd better do a bit of grocery shopping and head home.

Bill wanted to know if Lester's family had visited him since he had been in the hospital.

Lester said, "Yes, they were here last Sunday. It was pretty rough on Mother to see me all bandaged up, so they left early. They said they would be back when they could see my face. But that may shock them even more than the bandages if my surgeons can't fix my face back like it was before the accident. Dr. McKinley told me that due to the extent of the damage to my face and the fact that the infection was left untreated for so long, that it's very likely that I may not look like I did before the accident. So, I guess I'll know when it's finished."

They didn't have anything planned for Sunday, so they just rested and talked.

Bill said, "We'll go fishing in that small lake down there, next weekend. That is if you want to come back here with me for the weekend again."

Lester said, "I'd like that, if it's ok with my doctor. And Bill, I'm expecting some paperwork on my medical studies. If I get it before the weekend, I'd like to bring it along and study a little at your house that is if it's ok by you."

Bill said, "Sure. So, you are studying to be a doctor?"

Lester said, "I will be when I get the information. I thought since I'm going to be in the hospital for quite some time I may as well pick up where I left off on my studying."

Bill said, "Oh that's great!"

LET'S CHECK BACK WITH JUNE AND SEE IF SHE HAS ANY NEWS ABOUT HOLSTONE

JUNE WAS STILL WORKING ON HER QUEST for Holstone. She had gone to cemeteries, police stations, newspapers, hospitals, doctors' offices, clinics, homeless shelters, hobo camps, dumps along the railroad and river, to countless people she didn't know, and, so far, she had come up with nothing. The thought had crossed her mind to stop looking and just forget the whole thing.

But at the start of each new day, a thought came back into her mind. It was like a little voice whispering, "Keep looking. Don't give up now. You've put a lot of time and money in what you're doing, so don't stop now."

She said, "Ok little voice, give me some pointers, places to look, people to talk to, something new instead of all this advice that's getting me nowhere fast. It's costing me big bucks, working me to death and I still don't know any more than I did when I started. I've been working on it over two years."

June was having lunch in the little town of Venus when a stranger approached her and said, "I'm Nelson Phillips. I hear that you are looking for a relative that's been missing for a long time."

June said, "Yes I am."

Nelson said, "Don't get me wrong. I'm not doing this for money. I just want to help if I can. I saw your ad in the paper. When I'd seen you had come to town, I knew you must be the one that put the ad in the paper. I've lived here all my life and know just about everyone, since it's a small town. A stranger came here, a young boy about the time you say your half-brother was missing. He said he was sixteen, but he looked a lot younger, but that's neither here nor there. I think he said he was sixteen so he could get work. He was hired on down at the boat factory. Now I hear that he owns most of the factory. It might be worth checking into. His name is Andrew Henderson."

June thanked him and rushed through her lunch. Then, she rushed down to the boat factory. She walked into the office and asked for Mr. Henderson.

The well-dressed gentleman behind the desk with blond hair, blue eyes and fair skin said, "That would be me, so what can I do for you?"

June was saying to herself, "What do I do now. To be truthful, I'm not sure I'm ready for this." She couldn't think of anything to say.

Mr. Henderson said, "Well you must have come here for something. So, spill it. I'm a busy man, got a business to run.

June finally said, "I'm June. I'm looking for a half-brother of mine who disappeared several years ago. I thought that, uh, I mean that you might happen to uh maybe have known him, since I understand that you have been here a long time." Henderson said, "Well what's his name and what can you tell me about him? I'm not a detective, but if you tell me something about him then I might be able to help you out."

June said, "Well he disappeared before I was born and all I can tell you is what my mother has told me about him. He was twelve years old when he disappeared. He has, had, blond hair and blue eyes. I have a picture of him when he was ten or eleven."

Henderson took the picture, looked at it for a long time, handed it back to June and said, "I haven't seen anyone that looks like him around here. I'm sorry but that is all I can say. I'm not your man."

June took the picture and left his office. On the way to her car, she said to herself, "Mr. Henderson isn't dumb, that's for sure. If I'm not badly mistaken, I'm pretty sure his last words were, "I'm not your man.

"That told me he knew very well why I came to see him and what I was thinking. In my mind that doesn't weed him out because I noticed he looked at the picture of Holstone for quite some time before handing it back to me.

"I'm thinking he could still be brother Holstone. I'll just have to attack this little problem in another way. Now he is my best bet until I check deeper into who he really is and where he came from. I guess I could go back and pretend to be applying for a job and go from there from what I have found out.

"So, Mr. Henderson came here about the time brother Holstone went missing. He has blond hair and blue eyes. He fits the description of my missing brother.

"Of course, Mr. Henderson is the type of person that you don't push. He will tell you no more than he wants to. I can't find out where he came from but there are many more alleys I can check out."

THE MYSTERY MAN, MR. HENDERSON

AS NELSON PHILLIPS TOLD JUNE, Mr. Henderson had come to Venus as a very young boy. He walked into town, went to the boat factory, and asked the boss for a job. The boss was also the owner of the boat factory, Mr. Johnnie Cantrell. Cantrell told him that he didn't hire boys, just men who can work.

Henderson said, "Sir, I can handle any job that you have here to be done. All I ask is a chance."

Cantrell asked, "How old are you son?"

Henderson said, "I'm sixteen."

Cantrell said, "Now I know better than that."

The boy said, "I realize that I'm a little ragged and skinny. To tell you the truth, I haven't eaten a decent meal in several days. That's why I need a job."

Cantrell turned to go back into his office, then turned back and said, "I'll no doubt regret this. Can you sweep floors?"

Henderson said, "Yes sir. My name is Andrew Henderson. You will never regret this. I thank you so much from the bottom of my heart."

Cantrell said, "I take it that you don't have any money. I'll advance you a week's pay."

This young boy came to town from no one knew where. He didn't attend school. He lived at a boarding house a couple of days and realized his money was running out. Then he lived in an abandoned house just out of town.

The old house didn't have running water or electrical power. There was no furniture. Andrew slept on the floor and got his drinking water from the little creek that ran by the old

38

house. He used an old bucket he had found in the dump just outside of town to bring in the water. He cleaned up the best he could. He wanted to hold onto that job now that he had it. He knew that the other workers would be looking at him and he wanted to look the best he could under the circumstances. He thought, "You do what you have to do with what you have to do it." Without a doubt he knew hard times very well.

While he was sweeping floors, he took notice of all the other work that was going on with the boat building. One day one of the builders was sick and didn't show up for work. Henderson went to the boat and started to work on it.

Cantrell came running and said, "What do you think you're doing, boy?" He started to say, "Get back to your broom."

Then one of the other employees said, "Mr. Cantrell, if you don't mind me buttin' in, just watch him a few minutes. He does as good a job as anyone in here."

Cantrell let him work. At the end of the day, Cantrell came over to where Henderson was cleaning up.

Henderson said, "Well are you going to fire me for my misconduct?"

Cantrell said, "No, I'm going to give you a raise and put you on the builders list. Just one question. Where did you learn to do that type of work?"

Henderson said, "I just watched the workmen here and decided I could do the work."

Cantrell said, "You will go places my boy."

No one knew where Henderson came from and didn't know if Henderson was his real name.

He did his work well, stayed out of trouble. He never got any mail, didn't have a car. He didn't associate with anyone except at work. He did his grocery shopping late at night just before the store closed. He was a puzzlement to all that heard about him.

As already noted, the boy, or Mr. Henderson, came to the town of Venus with rags on his back, hungry and very much unkempt. He worked hard at his new job which he was so thankful to get. The other employees liked him and his work, although they couldn't figure him out. They just took him as who he was and what he did.

He saved his money and before long he had saved enough to purchase a few acres of land just outside of Venus, land that no one else wanted. It was hardly worth paying state taxes on. Since this land was out of the town limits, he didn't have to follow town rules. He built a makeshift one room shack on it, mostly from scrap wood he picked up from the throw away pile at the boat factory. He lived there without electricity, telephone, or heat except an old wood burning device that he had salvaged from a dump.

He wasn't a wasteful man, of course it's hard to waste when one doesn't have much to waste. He lived like this until he saved enough money to hire a contractor to build a house for him. Of course, he did quite a bit of the work on the house himself, or, as some in Venus called it, a mansion. The builders were the only ones that had ever been in it, and they were all from out of town. He lived in his own little world as much as possible.

It's believed that he came to the town of Venus at around the age of twelve. Telling by the condition he was in when Mr. Phillips first saw him it was very unlikely that he had very much education but that didn't seem to affect him in the least. He was no doubt a self-made and educated man. He knew how to get along and deal with people, to be liked and respected by all who knew him.

MONDAY MORNING ROLLED IN

DR. MCKINLEY SAID TO MCCLOUD, "May I call you Lester?"

McCloud said, "That's fine and it's shorter. So, I'll just be Lester while I'm here in this hospital."

McKinley said, "Then call me Jeff. Now I'll remove some of these bandages and have a look at your face. If the infection has cleared up, maybe we can do a little work today.

He removed some of the bandages from one side of Lester's face. He said, "It looks pretty good. It appears most of the infection has cleared up. On that note I think we can do some work today. Oh, I forgot to ask, did you have a good time over the weekend with the Rayes?"

McCloud said, "It was wonderful. They treated me like family. I enjoyed it more than I could ever tell you. The good thing is they have invited me back this coming weekend, if it's ok by you."

Dr. McKinley said, "It's ok with me unless we run into problems this week. So, if everything goes well with what we will be doing to your face, you go for the trip to the country. It will do you good to get out of here for a couple of days."

The week went well. The doctors accomplished quite a bit that week. Friday evening Bill rolled Lester's wheelchair out to the car and away they went to the country.

Bill said, "We'll rest tonight and go fishing tomorrow, if it's ok with you."

Lester said, "Can't wait for morning to get here."

Kathie fixed a big breakfast on Saturday morning. After eating breakfast, the men got their fishing reels and went to the lake.

Lester said, "This is a beautiful place, just a hop and a jump from the capitol. I would love to have such a place of my own when I retire from the Royal Air Force."

Bill said, "I couldn't afford this much land this close to town and in this state on my salary, if it hadn't been handed down to me from my family. It was handed down to my parents by their parents. Sometimes it seems like the taxes are getting so high that I wonder how long I'll be able to hold on to it. I get letters, phone calls and visitors just about every day or three wanting to buy the property. I could get a nice little chunk of money for it. But then where would my wife and I go?"

They didn't catch enough fish for lunch, but they did catch a couple. Since it was Saturday night, everyone put on their best and went to town for dinner and a movie.

Lester said, "You folks know how to live and enjoy yourself. For me I guess I've been in the fast lane for the past few years. Sometimes everything just seems to roll up in one big ball and almost runs me down.

"If I didn't have friends like you folks and Dr. Holt and of course my parents, I would really be lost in the twilight zone. Of course, the Air Force has given me a lot to look forward to and I do miss flying. I wonder sometimes if I'm going to be able to go back to my job as a pilot after my surgery is all completed.

"I've heard of some pilots that get injured while flying and the flight surgeon says they are not fit to fly. They're given a desk job to finish out their time to retirement. I don't want that. I'm just not a sit around kind of man, I like to be busy doing something. I realize flying almost cost me my life, but a person can get killed doing almost anything. Of course, if the war is still going on when I get out of the hospital, I'll more than likely go back to my flying job."

Sunday was a rest day. They just laid around, eating, and sleeping. Then he went back to the hospital Monday morning and more surgery. Lester had so many bandages on him where the doctor had removed skin, he looked like a patchwork quilt. The week went well on the surgery.

Lester's friend, Raye, came around and told him that he had weekend duty and that they wouldn't be going to the country this weekend.

Lester said, "That's fine by me, I've received some medical books that I need to get into and see what I need to do to carry on with my medical studies. This surgery will be over before I know it and since the war is still going on I'll be flying. I need to stay up to date on what I need to know. It's almost a full-time job.

JUNE IS STILL WORKING ON FINDING HOLSTONE

AFTER JUNE'S VISIT WITH MR. HENDERSON, at his mansion, the thought was running through her head that this Mr. Henderson could, just could, be her half-brother Holstone. Going on what Mr. Phillips said about this young boy coming to town alone several years ago and telling the owner of the boat factory that he needed work. He said that he was sixteen, but he looked about twelve years old. This young boy turned out to be Mr. Henderson.

He didn't resemble anyone in her family, but he did have blond hair and blue eyes. She had never seen her half-brother, just had a picture to go by. Talk got around that Dr. Holt might be Holstone' father. Now Holstone, the oldest kid in the family, was born out of wedlock. That was before June's father, Hector Wonderland, met June's mother, Alice Shannon. June wanted to ask her mother about this, but she didn't want to embarrass her with all these questions about another man besides her stepfather. But on the other hand, how else was she going to find out. She really did want to know.

She knew Dr. Holt wouldn't tell her anything if he knew. So, she would have to find out some other way or not at all. She thought about going back to talk with Mr. Henderson, but she couldn't think of any excuse to go to him because he seemed like the type of person that didn't waste much time on things that weren't profitable. It showed when you talked with him.

That's why he owned the boat factory because he didn't waste time with small talk and gossip. If it wasn't his business, he didn't waste time discussing it. He was a man that very few people knew anything about, but he was respected by all who knew him.

JUNE IS THINKING ABOUT STALKING HENDERSON

JUNE THOUGHT ABOUT HANGING AROUND THE TOWN and maybe going to some of the same places that Henderson went to and maybe he would ask her for a date. But then if he was in fact her half-brother she would be in trouble.

On that note she said to herself, "Forget that avenue."

June was on her way home to think about this and figure out more ways to look for Holstone. Then she thought of Mr. Phillips.

She thought, "I wouldn't really call him nosy. He just likes to keep up with things that are going on in Venus."

In that case he might be of help to her. She turned the car around and went back to Venus, thinking that Mr. Phillips shouldn't be too hard to find in a little burg like that. But then she didn't exactly know where to start.

June didn't know this, but Nelson Phillips owned the local hardware store in another town but lived in Venus. He kept to himself. The people of Venus only knew him by the name of Hawthorn. He seemed to keep up with all that was going on in Venus.

No one seemed to know why they called Mr. Phillips Hawthorn. June didn't know if that was his last or middle name or just a nick name that someone hung on him.

Since June wasn't sure in which town he owned a business, she went to the restaurant where she saw him before. She got a phone book, turned to the Ps, but no Nelson Phillips listed. Dead end there. She asked some of the people that worked at the restaurant if they knew a Nelson Phillips. No one knew.

June thought, "Well, since I'm asking questions, I may as well ask about Henderson."

The woman that owned the restaurant said, "I know him. He comes here almost every day for lunch. I know he is good looking, wealthy, owns controlling interest in the boat building business here. I know that he's a hard worker. Keeps to himself, single. I've never seen him with a woman except the two that come here with him sometimes for lunch. One of them is his secretary.

"I heard that he came here as a very young boy. He said he was sixteen so he could get a job. He was hired as a cleanup boy and now he owns controlling interest in the boat factory. He lives about five miles out of town in a two-story mansion valued at about one half million dollars. What else do you want to know about him?"

June said, "I guess that does, uh, about does it." June thought to herself, "I was lucky to get the time he gave me the other day."

Just as she was leaving in walked Mr. Henderson.

He recognized her and said, "So we meet again June. It is June, isn't it?"

She was so caught off guard she couldn't speak. He said, "Have a cup of coffee with me and get your voice back."

June thought to herself, "Don't mess this one up. Go for it and by all means have that cup of coffee with him. This is what you wanted, isn't it?"

Mr. Henderson said to the waitress, "My private booth please and two cups of coffee." June managed somehow to make it to the booth that Mr. Henderson indicated. He said, "Well what brings you back to Venus? Still looking for that missing half-brother of yours, I suppose. Have you any leads?"

June finally spoke and said, "No and I think the element of time has the upper hand here."

He said, "From what you told me it has been a long time. I'm sure most of the people that knew him are dead and gone."

June said, "Yes I suppose so, but I also have the feeling that someone knows something about my missing half-brother, if they would just open up and tell me. Since they haven't, that tells me someone is hiding something. But for what reason I haven't been able to figure out. Of course, most of this all depends on if he is still alive."

"Well, I'd help if I knew where to start. A private detective might be your best way of finding out something. Of course, a private detective can get expensive. You pay them by the hour, and you also pay them whether they find out anything or not." Henderson said.

All this time June was thinking about what her mother had told her about her father, Hector, using a stock whip on Holstone. June was thinking, "If I could see Mr. Henderson's back and arms, I could see if there are any scars from the whip. But how on earth am I going to do that? I'll have to run that through my mind several times and see if I can come up with an answer."

Mr. Henderson's words brought June out of her thoughts, as he was saying, "If you would like for me to ask around and see if I can find out anything, I would be more than glad to help. Just give me a few days. You could come back here say, oh, this is Tuesday, you could come back Friday evening. We could have dinner and I can tell you if I found out anything. Is that a deal?"

June said, "I'll be here."

June said to herself, "That must be more words than anyone has gotten from Mr. Henderson since he came to this town. Most people I've talked to tell me he says very little or nothing to anybody. So, I consider myself very lucky indeed. In fact, I think he likes me. But I must not get carried away with this, not just yet. No way will I tell anyone."

On her way home she was trying very hard to come up with a way to see Mr. Henderson's back, to see if there were any scars. She didn't want to push this invitation too far and frighten him away because she had really made quite a headway in such a short time. She figured that Mr. Henderson was a loner, just didn't have time for people, that is if it wasn't profitable. The rest of the week went slowly for June. She was anxious to see if Mr. Henderson found out anything about her half-brother and of course to see him again.

JAMES CODY, FROM THE GERMAN PRISON CAMP, IS COMING TO SEE LESTER

AS IT TURNED OUT, LESTER DIDN'T GET TO STUDY his medical textbook. During the week his prison camp friend, James Cody, called and asked if it would be ok to visit him on Sunday.

Lester said, "Of course, I would love to see you again."

Sgt. Cody arrived at the hospital early Sunday morning. In fact, he had breakfast with Lester, then dinner – the noon meal.

Lester said, "Tell me all about what happened to you at the prison rescue."

Cody said, "I was on my way to an opening that I had made in the fence earlier when I heard the helicopter coming. I wasn't sure just which side it was from. I wanted to come back and help others out, but it was too late for that. Since I didn't know who the helicopter belonged to, I decided to keep running. I didn't know if I'd get another chance or not. I was picked up later by the rescue team and at the time I was so weak and run down, I didn't know where I was or who picked me up. I was in the hospital at Wright-Paterson Air Force Base in Ohio for two weeks.

"I learned later three of our friends who were in prison with us were shot and killed during the rescue mission. Sgt. Delos Bradley and Maj. John L. Cummings, both real fine people, and the third one was Frank McHenry. I knew him but not that well. I'm really surprised there weren't more than that killed. Of course, the rescue was well planned and carried out by professionally trained people. So how is the surgery going?"

Lester said, "After the infection cured up the lacerations started healing. The doctors are working at least twelve hours a day on it, but it is slow going. From what they tell me I may have to get new credentials when this is all over because I won't look the same as before. That disturbs me. My parents were down to see me a couple of days ago and my mother was very upset to see me all bandaged up, so they left early. They said they would come back another time."

James asked, "How are you passing the time on weekends?"

Lester said, "One of the orderlies who takes care of me here, invited me to go home with him for two weekends. He is a very special friend to me. He's made my stay here so much easier for me. He had duty this weekend and that's why I'm here. Of course, after you called that you were coming to visit me this weekend, I would have told him that I'd pass on this weekend, because I wouldn't want to miss your visit."

Cody told Lester that he had received orders for an overseas assignment and would be leaving in about two weeks.

"I'll be going to England. With my specialty code as a special weapons operator, I'll be back in the war. But that's what we get paid to do."

Lester said, "Well I just hope that I'm fit for duty as a pilot when this surgery is finished because that's what I was trained for. It's really all I know how to do. Sure don't want a desk and pencil job. I wasn't trained for that."

Cody said, "Captain, Sir, I would like to hang around and have supper with you, but I guess I had better move along back to Wright-Patterson and see if assignments has any news for me on my assignment. I'll keep in touch pal, and you be careful if you go back to flying."

Lester said, "Since you're going to be assigned to a base in England if I get to go back to flying maybe I'll get to visit you there. As matter of fact, I could be stationed at the same base. Of course, this surgery is first. I can't cross two bridges at the same time. I'll just have to wait and see how it goes here but, in the meantime, we'll stay in touch.

MR. HENDERSON WAS WAITING FOR JUNE

MR. HENDERSON WAS WAITING FOR JUNE at the restaurant and stood up when June approached his private table. He held the chair for her and said, "Please sit down, Miss Wonderland."

June was wondering, "How does he know my last name? The best that I can remember when I introduced myself to him the first time we met, I only said, 'My name is June.' So that means that he has been asking folks questions about me. That's interesting."

After they finished their dinner, Mr. Henderson said, "Well I didn't find out anything about your half-brother. What I found out was that some folks don't know anything about him, and some are just not going to talk."

June said, "That's exactly what I have found out."

He said, "I normally don't get involved in this type of thing or give out advice. But I will say this to you. Don't burn yourself out over this. Just slow down and take it one step at a time. I'm not trying to pick you up, but I need to go home. You can come along if you're not afraid to be alone with me."

June said, "That's just fine with me, and no I'm not afraid to be alone with you."

When they walked in the doorway of the mansion, June thought, "My, my what a dwelling for just one person to live in."

Mr. Henderson said, "Make yourself at home while I make a few phone calls. There are drinks in the refrigerator. Help yourself. All my drinks are non-alcoholic. I don't use alcohol."

June thought, "No alcohol. Well, that means he didn't ask me out here to get me drunk then take advantage of me. So that's another plus."

She found a drink she liked and was looking around at the paintings in his study.

Mr. Henderson came in and said, "Most of these paintings were sent to me by friends from different parts of the world. They aren't worth much, but I don't show them to just anybody.

"As a matter of fact, I'm a loner. Some of my employees and my business partner have seen them but that's all. I get lonely out here sometimes, but I have my library and my job pretty well takes up most of my time. I don't have time to entertain people. Come this way and have a look at my library."

June said to herself, "I have never seen so many books in one place."

Mr. Henderson said, "If you see something you would like to read, take it with you, and, of course, return it when you're finished. Come this way. I had this house built to my liking ten years ago. It's more room than I need and probably ever use but it was what I wanted. Do you live with your parents, June?"

She said, "Yes, most of the time, except when I work, I stay with a friend over in Johnson. When I work it's just too far to drive home for a few hours' sleep and go again. It doesn't pay me to rent an apartment since I don't work full time. I can stay at home with my parents a lot cheaper. But I do realize that the day is coming when I'll have to be totally on my own and at that time, I'll need to get a full-time job. But currently a part-time job is perfect for me. It gives me the time I need to look for my half-brother. Some folks think I'm wasting my time, but it's what I think I should do and what I want to do. Besides, I have this weird feeling that he is still alive, and I really think that I'll see him one day.

Mr. Henderson said, "I'm sure you will if he is still alive because you are very determined and you have faith beyond anyone that I have ever known. If you didn't think so, then you wouldn't be spending all this time and money trying to find him. He's been gone for so long and you've never seen him except a photograph of him when he was about twelve years old. Do you think you would recognize him if you met him on the street? That brings up the thought that he could be walking around here, and you have seen him but didn't know him."

June said, "Yes, I have thought of that. I've wondered myself if I would recognize him. I tell you what would really kill me is if I found out that he is walking around here laughing at me for spending all this time and hard-earned money searching for him. Now that would really put me in a foul mood. But I don't think that would be the case

LESTER WILL SOON BE DISCHARGED FROM THE HOSPITAL

DR. MCKINLEY CAME IN TO HAVE A CHAT with Lester. He said, "You are doing very well with the surgery. The other doctors, and I have done just about all that's necessary. The healing will take a few more weeks. It will be almost like it was before the accident, the only thing is, as I'm sure you already know, you won't look the same as you did before the accident. As a matter of fact, people that you knew before will most likely not recognize you now. I know without a doubt that news disturbs you beyond words and it bothers me too to have to tell you such news, but I thought it my duty to inform you. Especially since I'm one of the doctors doing the work on you."

All this time, Lester was thinking, "If it's got to be this way, I could go back to the old home place and have a look around and no one would recognize me. But, on the other hand, if I did get the notion to do that it wouldn't be in the near future. Just a thought I guess."

His mind was jogged back to reality by Dr. McKinley's saying, "Lester I'll be back in a couple of hours with your discharge papers and instructions for you on how you need to take care of the work we have done on your face and hand." A couple of hours went by, then Dr. McKinley came in with a handful of paperwork.

He said, "I have the ok from your unit to give you a thirty-day convalescent leave. After that, if you're doing ok, no infection, no pain, and if the surgery looks good to you, I'd like you to go to the doctor and or flight surgeon and let them have a look. As for me I don't see any reason why you can't go back to flying if you want to. If you need to talk to me at any time my phone number is on one of these forms I'll give you. You'll spend the night here. You're free to go tomorrow. Good luck with your flying Capt. McCloud."

McCloud called his parents and gave them the good news. He said, "Come and take me home please."

The thirty-day leave passed swiftly. The flight surgeon gave him a clean bill of health and an ok to return to flying. He felt like a new man returning to his old unit. He was welcomed by all. To his surprise no one mentioned that he looked different. But it had been a long time since any of them had seen him.

Six months later he was assigned to a squadron in England. He said to himself, "It's back into the war again, but that's what I was trained to do. If I would admit it, it's what I really want to do."

When he wasn't flying, he was in his books studying for his medical exam. He had been getting good reports on his work so far, but due to his accident and long stay in the hospital, it was all done on paper and mailed in. He realized he had a long way to go but he was still a young man and very determined to get what he wanted. He was in the right place to do it.

One night while Lester was stationed in England, when most everyone was sleeping after a long day of flying, he thought he heard a plane pass over the barracks real low and quiet. He dressed quickly and went outside. He realized it was early in the morning. He looked at his watch and saw it was one-thirty a.m. Then he heard the airplane again. It was flying at tree top altitude. He could see the German insignia on the side of the plane. Just behind it was another one of the same type. He ran back into the barracks, grabbed his helmet, ran out half-dressed, jumped in his airplane, fired it up, and headed for the runway. He knew the two German pilots were looking for the best place to drop their bombs, where they would do the most damage.

McCloud left the runway without any lights on his airplane hoping he could get in the air before the German pilots saw him. He hoped to surprise them with a little aircraft fire. It took him a little while to find the two planes. At first, he thought they had left the area, but just then he spotted one of them flying over the parked aircraft. He took his time and waited to see what this pilot was going to do. He didn't want to shoot him down over the airfield or housing. So, he waited, and it worked. He got behind one of the aircraft and shot it down, no doubt without the pilot ever knowing he was there. The second pilot was a different story. While McCloud had been busy with the first plane, the second pilot saw what was going on and eased behind him without him knowing, just as McCloud did with the first. The German pilot began to fire on McCloud. Several bullets hit his plane. He realized his plane was losing power and the fuel indicators were showing a loss of fuel. He knew it was now or never if he was going to put this German plane in the dirt. He made his move and it worked. He made his way to where he could get a shot at the side of the German plane. He let go with everything he had. The enemy aircraft went up in smoke. But McCloud had a problem. He had a fire in the tail section of his aircraft. He pushed the fire extinguisher button and waited but nothing happened. He put his plane into a dive. Sometimes that will blow the fire out, but this wasn't one of those times. His next option was to bail out and let the plane aft go. He had been so engrossed in all that had happened in the last thirty minutes that he wasn't sure if he was over friendly territory or not and he wasn't very sure he could make it back to his base with all that was going on.

So, he got on the radio and said, "I'm on fire and bailing out."

Base radio operator said, "I'll send rescue to find you."

Rescue found him with no problem. When he arrived at the base, the wing commander, the base commander, and his squadron commander were all waiting for him. He hadn't realized it, but he was still wearing only his pajamas and slippers.

The wing commander said, "Where in the world have you been Captain?"

He replied, "Just defending the base and country, Sir."

His squadron commander said, "Let's go inside and you can tell us what happened."

McCloud said, "I need to get into proper attire."

The commander said, "If you can fly an airplane and shoot down, I assume, two German planes while wearing those clothes, then I think you can give your report to us in the same clothes."

Lester gave them a short explanation of what happened.

He said, "I'm sorry I lost the plane."

The squadron commander said, "You get some rest and give us a detailed report tomorrow. You have done enough for today."

In McCloud's written report he stated that he awoke at about one thirty a.m. to what sounded like an aircraft engine running with mufflers on it.

At first, I thought I was dreaming, but then I heard it again. And it sounded closer this time. I also realized that I wasn't asleep as I had thought. I put on my robe and went outside to have a look and listen. Then the aircraft appeared just above the treetops. It was so close I could read the German insignia on the side of the aircraft.

"I ran back into the barracks and grabbed my helmet. I didn't realize I still had on my pajamas. I ran to my aircraft, taxied out and took off without any lights. I was hoping the German pilots wouldn't see me, and I think it worked. I got behind one of them right off and fired on him. The aircraft went to the ground. I think the other one was looking for the best place to drop his bombs.

"I was so engrossed in my work I didn't realize the other plane was right behind me until he began firing on me. I knew my aircraft had been hit in the tail section. My fuel gages were going to the low side too fast, so I realized I had been hit in the wing area also. I needed to do what I was going to do fast. I managed to get a side view of him, and I let him have everything I had. As I watched his aircraft head for the ground, I realized I couldn't reach the base without fuel. I stayed with it as long as I could and got myself a little closer to the base. Before I bailed out, I was able to call rescue and they found me.

Captain Lester J. McCloud
Royal Canadian Air Force

Squadron Commander Lester Mathew called McCloud in and said "That was a very good report Captain. By being alert and following through with what you knew you had to do, I'm sure you saved many lives, several aircraft and the base. I will see to it that you are recognized for this."

The next promotion cycle Captain McCloud was promoted to the rank of Major.

The squadron commander called him in and said, "Major McCloud, there is an opening in the squadron for a flight leader. I would like to see you get that job. I know you can handle the job and will do your best. And congratulations on the promotion."

Major McCloud said, "Let me think about this position. It's a lot more work, not to speak of the responsibility. When you assign these pilots to a mission you never know if they'll come back or not. Most of them have families. I'll give it my best thoughts. Thanks again for thinking of me."

After two days had passed, Major McCloud, reported back to his Squadron Commander and said "I've given this job offer a lot of thought. I realize that if you didn't need the job filled then you wouldn't have asked me to take it, so I'll do the best that I can with it."

Colonel Mathew said, "You'll make it work. Thanks a lot. You've made my job a lot easier."

Major McCloud looked over the names of all the pilots in the squadron, he needed a second, someone to take over when he wasn't available.

He called a meeting with all the pilots two hours prior to mission take off time. Since he was a new man to the squadron and appointed to the new job, he needed to learn more about the fliers he would be dealing with. He needed their thoughts about what they were doing, how they felt about the mission they would be asked to do, any negative thoughts about what they were asked to do. He needed to know all these things about the men he was dealing with, and of course maybe select a second person for the job he was doing.

In the briefing room Major McCloud said, "Good morning gentlemen, I'm Major McCloud your new flight commander. I called this meeting a bit early because I wanted to learn a little bit about the pilots I'll be flying with while I'm here in England. I'll admit to you guys that I pulled a stupid move a few nights ago when I ran out of my quarters alone to fight with a couple of German aircraft. Which brings me to say this, if you see the German air force while on a mission and get into a shooting match with them, let some of the glory go to your wing men, or vise-versa. Don't try to do it all alone like I did. It was a stupid move I made, and I'll admit it. End of lecture on that subject. That's all I have for today. Just be careful out there. Captain Evince I'd like to see you in my office for a moment."

Major McCloud told Evince, "I'm looking for a good second, someone to fill in when I can't be here. I've looked over your records. I think you'll do a good job. It would please me very much if you would consider taking the job. You would be a lot of help to me because you know the pilots much better than I do. Think about it as you fly today and let me know. Thanks, and that will be all for now. Have a good safe flight."

The 322nd Royal Canadian Air Force Fighter Squadron had sixteen fighter aircraft and twenty-one pilots. Most of the missions they were assigned to called for five sometimes seven aircraft. At times they would join with the American fliers.

The 322nd squadron had a good flying record, but the war was getting heavy with German aircraft and bigger guns from the ground. Major McCloud announced that next week they would be teaming up with the Americans on a very important mission which would require all the planes that the 322nd had. It happened that next week was two days away.

On this mission the Germans were waiting for them. They must have gotten the word somehow. The Americans lost three aircraft and the 322nd lost two.

McCloud said to himself, "This is the hardest part of this job, notifying the families of the lost pilots." It was a heart-breaking job, but someone had to do it.

He called Captain Evince in his office and said, "I need your help on this matter of writing to the families of the pilots we lost today. Since you were there, you know more about what happened than I do. Fill me in on the particulars and I'll write the letters."

Captain Evince said, "You are new here sir and I've been with this squadron for quite a while. If I'm going to be second in command, it's time that I do my first job as your second. With your permission, sir, I'll write the letters."

Major McCloud replied, "Welcome aboard and many thanks Captain."

When Colonel Mathew knocked on Major McCloud's door, he said, "Come in."

The colonel had two cups of coffee in his hands.

He said "I thought you could use some company and a cup of what they call coffee around here. I hear that you picked Captain Evince as your second, good selection. He's a good officer and he'll do his best.

"Looks as though we've lost two pilots. I was hoping that someone would have seen a chute and that rescue might have been able to pick them up before the Germans got to them. I've questioned all pilots that were on this mission, plus, I called the American squadron. But no one saw a chute. With the war building up I guess it's to be expected. A thing like this is never easy, and it's hard to know just what to say when you have to notify the family. If you need some help in that area, feel free to ask."

Major McCloud replied, "Captain Evince volunteered to take care of the job."

Colonel Mathew said, "I see by your records that your plane was shot down over Germany some time back. Want to talk a little about it?

Major McCloud replied, "I'll tell you what I know. I was a young flier and really wasn't ready for air combat especially with experienced pilots like the Germans. I just got careless. It shouldn't have happened. After I was shot out of the air the Germans found me in a field. They wouldn't have found me if I hadn't been cut up pretty badly. My face was cut to pieces and my left hand was really torn up. I was bleeding so bad from the damage done to my face that I couldn't see very well. I just didn't know which way to go. I had lost my pocket compass. They took me to a prison camp, and I didn't see a doctor for three days. By that time my wounds had gotten infected. The doctors don't get in a hurry in a prison camp. I'm not real sure just how long I was in the camp when the rescue team hit the prison early one morning. They wiped out all the guards, cooks, and bottle washers then rescued all the prisoners except, I believe, three that were killed either from German gun fire before they were all wiped out or if they were accidentally killed by stray shots from someone from the rescue team. I was taken to Walter Reed Hospital. Dr. McKinley and his crew put me back together. That's about it."

Colonel Mathew said "You have a very clean and interesting record. There's a unit at another base here in England. I've learned it needs a commanding officer. Would you be interested? If so, I'll recommend you. Your record speaks for itself. I really don't want to let you go, but this commander position would almost guarantee a promotion as soon as your time in grade time is up. It's a lot of responsibility but that's what we get paid for. You can be a squadron commander and still fly your missions just as you do here."

McCloud asked, "What happened to the officer that was commander of the squadron up to now?" Colonel Mathew said his time was up over here and he rotated.

JUNE IS THINKING ABOUT A BETTER PAYING JOB

JUNE WAS THINKING ABOUT A JOB other than the one she had. The one she was thinking about offered more money and time off to look for her half-brother. With more money coming in she might be able to hire a private investigator. One thing for sure she wasn't getting anywhere fast on her own.

When June met with Mr. Henderson the next time he said, "I've a proposition for you. I'm gone from home a lot in my work, sometimes two weeks at a time. That means my house is just standing there alone, open to anyone who wants to break in and take what they want. It's out in the country away from town and since I'm out of the city limits the city police don't go out that far.

"So, I'm offering you a job no strings attached. You take care of the house and cook the meals. You will have your own room. Your job will be, more or less, a caretaker. Oh, there would be talk of course about a woman living in, but that's all it would be is talk. You don't have to give me an answer just now. Think about it and let me know pretty soon."

June asked. "Why are you doing this for me? You don't know me that well."

Lester said, "I think I'm a pretty good judge of character, and I've asked around and talked to some people that know you. I think I can trust you with my home, especially since I'm paying you to do a job for me. Besides, you no doubt are spending most of what you make in searching for your half-brother, so a bigger paycheck would no doubt help out."

June left for home. On the way she thought of nothing else. She could see drawbacks to it but also pluses. One drawback would be the word getting around that she was living with a man and not married to him. It would be a lie, but people always seem to see things in the worst light and people do love to gossip. It's very hard to tell people how things really are when they want to hear and think the worst. She discussed this with her mother.

Her mother said, "Go for it. Let people talk if they want to. If they are talking about you then they are giving someone else a break. By the way June, I told myself I'd never breathe this to anyone, but since you are working so faithfully trying to find one half-brother, you may as well look for two of them.

June said, "My God Mother, what on earth are you talking about?"

Her mother said your half-brother has a twin. His name is Tom. He disappeared before Holstone did. They were both down at the river fishing and some railroad workers came along and were harassing them. Holstone came running to the house and by the time we arrived back at the river everybody was gone. I reported it to the police, but they were so slow getting here everybody had disappeared including Tom. We lived in another state at the time. I didn't have a job, nor a husband and times were hard. There just wasn't any money to hire an investigator. Tom's last name was Mansfield, and so was Holstone's, but your father adopted him and gave him a new name. Now the only one who knows about Tom is me, Holstone, and now you. So, let's keep it that way, shall we?"

June went back to have a talk with Mr. Henderson. She had a heavy load on her mind.

She was saying to herself, "How did I get into this mess anyway? I can't even get a lead on Holstone, let alone Tom."

She thought better about telling Mr. Henderson her mother had told her that she now had another half-brother to look for.

"At least for now," she thought, "I'll hold onto it and think about it until I decide what is best to do. The trail is so cold it's hardly a trail anymore."

She thought, "This job will give me more time to think this situation over before I get in over my head and look like a fool."

Then her mind went back to the business at hand. After all it was the paycheck that she needed.

She asked Henderson, "How much does the job pay. What do I need to know about things that need to be done on a daily or weekly basis, phone numbers of who I need to call in case something goes wrong at the house, and who purchases the groceries?"

He said, "I think you are honest and know better than try to get away with more than I'll be paying you, that is if you take the job."

June said, "I'll do my best. When do I start?"

Mr. Henderson said, "Be here Monday morning and I'll show you around and try to point out the things that need to be checked each day, how different things operate, and of course you will need an advance on your salary. I have a credit account at the grocery. I'll take you down there and introduce you to the owner and whoever else is on duty, so you shouldn't have any problem there."

She was at his house early Monday morning, in working clothes and carrying baggage.

Mr. Henderson said, "Let's go to the grocery and get that cleared for you in case you need to purchase something from there while I'm gone."

He then showed her the things around the house that needed to be looked after on a daily basis.

Then he said, "See you in about a week if everything goes as planned."

After Mr. Henderson was gone, June looked around the house and set up a schedule for herself to go by in order not to miss anything. The house wasn't huge, but it did cover quite a spread of land, two stories, a full basement, four bedrooms, and six baths.

She said to herself, "I can handle this situation and do all the thinking that I need to do on my search."

She wasn't nosy but she did look through a few things that she was sure she wasn't supposed to see. From what she could find and figure out Mr. Henderson came here as a stranger, as Nelson Phillips had said, with no more than the clothes on his back and just a kid.

"Now he owns controlling interest in the boat building business, lives in a mansion just outside of town," June thought to herself, "and is paying me very well to look after the mansion."

She had been running the information about Tom over and over in her mind.

She said to herself, "A thing like this can give a person brain burn. It's difficult to get a private investigator to look into a case of a missing person when you don't have a picture to go by. And he was twelve years old when he went missing. People do change as they grow up, and sometimes look so much different than when they were young. I must give this one a lot of thought before I'll consider spending money and time on it. Lord God only knows what the guys that grabbed him did to and with him."

June had finished her chores for the day early and was thinking about what her mother had told her about her other half-brother, Tom, that he disappeared before Holstone did, then the story Mr. Phillips told her about Henderson coming into town when he was about twelve years old. Now she needed to know what year Mr. Henderson came into town. If it was on or about the same year that Holstone went missing, then it might be something to look into.

June was beginning to think that Mr. Henderson could be her other missing brother, Tom. Now how on earth was she going to go about finding out? One thing for sure Mr. Henderson wouldn't tell her. A sneaking notion jumped into her head.

She said to herself, "It's mean of me to accept a wage from this man and go through his personal belongings while he's gone on the road making money to pay me, but I don't know any better way of finding out if he is who I think he might, or could, be. But Lord what will I do if I find out that he is my half-brother, Tom? If I had good sense, I'd drop this whole thing, and never think about it again, but some unknown thing is driving me on. I really don't know what it is, or where it's coming from, I guess that I'm sure it will pay off in the end."

June was thinking too much on this one thing, and just might get herself into trouble by being nosy. It could cause her to lose her job, but curiosity was getting the best of her. She started looking around and sticking her nose in things that weren't for her to see. The thing was about this man, as Mr. Phillips told June, Henderson came here with just the clothes on his back. If he was about twelve years old then he most likely didn't have a Social Security number or any documents that would have his date of birth on them, most likely just the credentials he carried in his wallet.

When Mr. Henderson returned from his trip June took off a couple of days. She went home to have a talk with her mother about Tom. She wanted to know from her mother if Tom had a birth certificate or anything that might give her a lead on her quest. Her mother told her that as far as she knew there was no paperwork at all on Tom.

"I didn't get a birth certificate on the twins because they cost money that I didn't have. Sorry June but that was just the way it was."

June said, "Well, I'll try and find Nelson Phillips, the gentleman that first told me about Mr. Henderson and see if he can, or will give me any information on Mr. Henderson, that is if he knows any more than what he already told me."

She went back to Venus. She had her own key to the mansion, as she opened the door the phone rang it was Mr. Henderson.

He said, "I'll be home in about two hours, fix us a good meal. I'm hungry for some good seafood."

June went in and checked the refrigerator just to make sure. There was seafood enough for two. She had forgotten that seafood was on the list of groceries that Mr. Henderson had ordered while she was off for those two days. When Mr. Henderson arrived home, dinner was ready. June set the table for Mr. Henderson and asked if she was to dine with him or, in the small kitchen.

Mr. Henderson said, "Nonsense, you are to dine with me."

June said, "I was just making sure, because some maids take their meals in the kitchen after they have served the family of the house."

Mr. Henderson said, "That's one of the reasons I hired you is because I don't like to eat alone. When I eat it seems the food stops about halfway down, and it doesn't seem to digest properly.

"I don't seem to ever get enough seafood," he added.

During the meal they chatted about things that were going on in the world. June had several questions she wanted to ask him, but just didn't have the nerve. After all he was her employer, and it just didn't seem proper to ask the questions that she wanted to know about. On her day off, which was a Saturday, June went to the restaurant.

She thought, "I asked about Mr. Phillips here before but maybe today someone else will be on duty at the restaurant that will know who I'm asking about."

As she went looking for Nelson Phillips, she went to the restaurant where she had first seen him.

The waitress there said, "Yes I think I know who you're asking about, but I think he goes by another name. Right off hand I can't think of that name. As I said I know him, but I haven't seen him in quite some time. He lives at the boarding house down at the end of Fifth Street West."

June left the restaurant and headed for the boarding house.

The woman at the boarding house said, "I think he's in his room. You are welcome to ring his doorbell and see if he'll answer. He doesn't stay here full time, kind of in and out."

June walked down the hallway to the last room in the building and knocked on the door several times. Minutes passed.

June was just about to give up and leave when the door opened and a man's voice asked, "What can I do for you? Oh, it's the lady who was inquiring about Andrew Henderson. Pardon my rudeness. Do come in."

June thanked him and walked past him into the room.

He said, "Well, did you find your man?"

June said, "Yes and he is a very nice person. I work for him now. I hope what I'm going to ask you won't make you think badly of me and that I'm sneaking around spying on the man I work for."

He said, "Fire away. I'll tell you what I know which isn't much. But sometimes not much is just what a person needs to close a case."

June asked, "Do you remember what year it was when Mr. Henderson came into town as a boy?"

Phillips said, "Yes I do remember. In fact, I write down unusual things that happen around here in my little book. One never knows when someone like you will come around asking about such things."

He gave her the date he had written down.

As she left, she said to herself, "Now I'm going to mother again and confirm the date that Holstone left the house."

When June arrived at home her mother asked, "Well, did you find out anything?"

June said, "Oh yes, but now I need more information from you. Do you remember when Tom disappeared?"

Her mother said, "The best that I can remember it was about three months before your father and I married. Tom was different from Holstone. Although they were twins, they were very different from each other, especially in the way they thought. Tom wasn't a boy to take orders from someone he didn't know and wasn't sure if they knew what they were talking about. He was what I would call a self-made person and could achieve anything that he wanted to. If it could be accomplished, he would accomplish it. Now Holstone was different in some of those ways but was pretty much the same in some as Tom was. I remember one time we were standing in the yard and a fleet of airplanes came flying over, training missions I suppose.

Holstone said, 'I could fly one of those things if given the chance.' He also liked to create things. I remember one time he built a model airplane. I never knew where he got the pattern from because I don't know that he ever saw a real airplane except the ones that would fly over the house from time to time. He built this model airplane from scrap wood he had found in a drift down by the river. I think it was too heavy to use for building airplanes. From what I understand, model airplanes are made from light weight wood.

That boy would have done well in the world if he had of lived. I shouldn't have worded it that way for I keep hoping he is alive somewhere in the world. But if so, something went wrong somewhere, something that we are unable to figure out. I don't know how true it is, but I've heard that there are people out there that grab up young kids and sell them to folks in foreign countries like slaves. If that's true and they did grab Holstone, I keep hoping that he will get a chance to get away sometime and return home. But it's been a long time now. Now don't you give up on trying to find them, because of what I said. You must keep trying to locate the boys.

JUNE RETURNS TO HER JOB

JUNE RETURNED TO HER JOB as housekeeper for Mr. Henderson. He met her at the door and said, "Welcome back home. I've missed you. Let's have dinner together again tonight and talk about your investigation."

To her surprise he had dinner almost ready.

She thought, "I wonder if he can see into the future? And I wonder if he knew I was on my way home and almost here. So, he prepared dinner for two?"

After dinner he said, "Well did you find out anything about your brother?"

She said, "Not really. It just seems like the same old thing day in and day out. If I didn't have so much time and money in this search I'd throw in the towel and say well, I tried."

He said, "Speaking of a towel after we finish dinner we can go for a swim if you are not afraid to be in the pool with me. That is if you have a bathing suit."

June said, "Great, I'd love that."

She was thinking to herself, "Now maybe I can get a good look at his back and that will tell me if he is or is not Holstone.

She was so excited about maybe getting to see Mr. Henderson's back that she forgot that she was also supposed to be looking for her other brother Tom, who had disappeared around the same time as Holstone.

At the swimming pool June got a good look at Mr. Henderson's back. It was just about like any other back and no scars as she could see. Then, all of a sudden, she realized that she didn't have any particulars on Tom. But she didn't think Tom would have scars on his back.

So, she told herself, "Turn one stone at a time. Just enjoy the warm water and the company of Mr. Henderson for the time being."

After the swim they went to the study and read a bit.

June said, "I've never seen so many good books all in one place before now."

Mr. Henderson said, "I've been collecting them for several years, in fact, ever since I arrived here. Do you have many books at home?"

June said, "Just a few, nothing to brag about. To tell you the truth we couldn't afford good books, but we do use the public library."

Mr. Henderson said, "Anytime when you go home on your day off you are welcome to take some of these home with you."

June said, "Thanks and good night," then went to her room.

June was up at dawn the next morning. After breakfast Mr. Henderson went to work and June started her day with the house chores.

McCLOUD DECIDES TO TAKE THE JOB AS SQUADRON COMMANDER

MAJOR MCCLOUD WENT TO COMMANDER MATHEWS and said, "I'll take the job as commander of that squadron, but first I'm due a thirty-day leave. I'll take the leave before taking the job."

Colonel Mathews said, "That's the thing to do. Oh, by the way, the squadron is the 207th Fighter Squadron. You enjoy your leave and I'll help the folks out at the 207th until you return."

When McCloud reached home, he called his dear friend Dr. Holt and asked him to join him and his family in Canada.

Dr. Holt said, "I need a vacation, so I'll be right up."

Major McCloud met Dr. Holt at the airport, they went home and had a good evening of rest.

Major McCloud said, "I'm Lester while here on leave."

John and Betty were so pleased to have their son home from the war, and a visit from Dr. Holt. It was always a pleasure to visit with him.

Lester told them all about his prison rescue again, and all about the folks that he had come in contact with during that time, and about the new position as Squadron Commander when he returned to England.

Lester said, "I've come in contact with so many wonderful folks since I've joined the Royal Air Force. That's put me to thinking, that is if it's ok with you Mother and Dad, when this war is over, I'd like to invite all of them to our town for a gathering."

Both parents said that it was a wonderful idea.

John said, "Since I'm principal of the school here, we could use it, that would give everyone plenty of room, and facilities, plenty of parking since it sounds like there will be several carloads of folks, if they all come. I'm hoping that you've made and kept a list of names and addresses of all the folks."

Lester said, "I did, and as far as I know they are all Americans. They were all so good to me not to speak of saving my life. I just thought it would be good to see them again. The pilots who flew the helicopters and rescued all of us from the prison camp in Germany, I never got to see their faces. The crews landed those helicopters in a hail of bullets. Even before the helicopter landed the swat team was out and firing at whatever moved that had a weapon in its hands. Talk about brave, well-trained men, I have no doubt they knew their jobs well. One thing for sure they saved all of us from no telling what, mainly something I would guess pretty close to Hell. God bless every last one of them for a job well done."

MAJOR McCLOUD'S THIRTY-DAY LEAVE IS UP BEFORE HE REALIZES IT

THE MAJOR HEADED BACK TO THE BASE where he would get orders for his job as squadron commander. When he arrived in England, the war was still very hot.

His stand in, Captain Albright, said, "Major, sir, we have been having a run of bad luck. We have lost an average of one airplane per day in the last ten days."

McCloud said, "Well let's have a look see into this situation and find the cause of this losing streak. First, how about the pilots of these downed planes, did any of them get out of their planes and make it back to the base?"

Albright replied, "Four, Major."

McCloud said, "Four out of ten did you say?"

Albright said, "Yes sir."

McCloud replied, "Call the four pilots in and let's see what we can find out from them as to why this is happening. Oh, by the way, I want to question them one at a time, one on one. We must get to the bottom of this thing before we are out of airplanes and pilots. Pardon me for not asking if you were one of the pilots that bailed out."

Albright said, "No, I've been lucky so far."

"Oh, Captain, see to it that the personnel files of these pilots are placed on my desk. I'd like about an hour to look over them before I start asking questions."

The first pilot he interviewed was Lieutenant Adrian Chasiter.

McCloud said, "Have a seat, can I get you a cup of coffee?"

Chasiter said, "Yes, thanks,"

Major McCloud said, "Lieutenant I guess you know by now that I'm your Squadron Commander. First things first, I understand you were shot down over the war zone."

Chasiter replied, "Yes sir."

Major McCloud asked, "Were you hurt when you bailed out?"

Chasiter replied, "Just a little damage to my right leg. I'm still not released for duty. The flight surgeon said I could go back to flying in another three days."

McCloud said, "That's good news. Now we will get right down to the business at hand. This meeting isn't going to damage anyone's career. It's to try to find out what is wrong, and why this squadron is losing pilots and airplanes at a record number. So, tell me all about the mission this incident happened in. Start from the time that you finished your breakfast, to the time you were shot out of the air. And let's hear it all."

Chasiter said, "After breakfast we, that's four of the pilots, went to briefing by Captain Albright. That lasted about thirty minutes. The mission was to destroy a shipyard somewhere in Germany, or as much of it as we could destroy with four airplanes. What we knew of it from briefing was that there was very little in the line of guarding it at that time of day. But one never knows. We were told to hit hard and move fast heading home. We were to fly as low as possible until we were in sight of the target, climb to twenty thousand feet, drop our load and make a beeline for home fast. But we never made it to where we could see the target. I guess I should say I never made it to where I could see the target and or start my climb. I believe flying low is what got us in dutch. Somewhere along the way we were spotted, and the word was passed on up ahead. Gunners were waiting and ready for us. No fault of Captain Albright. In fact, he has been doing a wonderful job since the Squadron Commander rotated. Two of the other six airplanes were hit with ground fire but not to the point that it downed them. The left wing of my airplane was shot off and it started to spin. I was so low to the ground I was very lucky to get out in time and get my chute opened before I made contact with the ground. As it was, I still hit pretty hard."

Major McCloud hadn't touched his coffee while the Lieutenant was giving his report. He finally asked, "What would you recommend Lieutenant? Since you have been doing the flying out there that puts you in a position to see more of what's going on, more than I know at this time."

Chasiter said, "First of all, I'd change the flight pattern, fly at a higher altitude. I'd use a different route for each mission although it would take a little more time to get there, but better late than not at all."

Major McCloud said, "That's something to think about. And I thank you for your report. Send in Lieutenant Brad Coffell."

Coffell knocked on the door and was invited in.

McCloud said, "Have a seat Lieutenant. Care for a cup of coffee?"

Coffell said, "Yes, thanks."

McCloud said, "I'm your new Squadron Commander. I'm also a fighter pilot. With that said, tell me about your mission: getting shot out of the air; what you think happened; what could have been done to keep a thing like this from happening. That's the purpose of this briefing, to find out what went wrong and what can be done about it if anything. This squadron is losing pilots and airplanes faster than the pilots can be trained and faster than the airplanes can be built. It's just got to slow down."

Coffell said, "Right after breakfast we went to the briefing room. Captain Albright briefed us on what we were supposed to hit on that mission. We were briefed on the target which was believed to be an ammo dump, or ammo holding depot. That was just me and my wing man, Lieutenant Jeff Lavish. We had been flying for about thirty minutes, when out of the clouds came four German fighters. These airplanes are bigger, faster, and from what we have learned, carry more fuel than we do. That gives them more airtime than us, and I might add the advantage. Anyway, they were right on top of us before we realized what was going on. They were shooting at us from overhead. I made a hard nose downturn hoping to get away from them and put myself in a position to get a gun sight on one of them. It worked, I came back up from his underside and gave him a blast of both guns. His airplane exploded all over me. If that wasn't enough, one of the other German airplanes made a pass at me while I was still blinded from the fire and smoke from the airplane I had just shot down. When my eyes got to where they could focus, I realized my airplane was on fire. As soon as I could find the ejection handle for the canopy, I pulled it and then I went out. Just in time I might add. In my opinion Sir, this could have happened to anyone. It's just one of those things that goes with the mission."

McCloud said, "Thank you Lieutenant, send in Lieutenant John Bear."

A little tap sounded on the door.

McCloud said, "Enter."

Lieutenant Bear matched his name. He filled the doorway.

McCloud said, "I have a coffee for you. Have a seat. As you probably know by now, I'm the new Squadron Commander here. Well Lieutenant I guess you know why you are here, so we will get right to the core of this thing. This squadron can't go on losing pilots and airplanes at the rate it's been going. So, let's see what we can do about it together. If you will, tell me everything that went on from briefing on that morning that you had your problem."

Lieutenant Bear said. "We were briefed, that was Lieutenant Moses and me, on a target, that as far as I know no one had hit yet, a small operation that builds aircraft parts. Our takeoff was set for two thirty a.m. The target was twenty minutes from base here. We made our delivery just fine and thought we were safe from any action from the Germans. But then, out of nowhere, came a half dozen German fighter planes. We had a hell of a fight until my fuel started getting dangerously low, but with six German planes on me and my fuel low I couldn't tuck tail and run. In other words, I was between a rock and a hard place. I was about to leave my wing man, Lieutenant Moses, and fight with six German aircraft. At about that time I think all six were after me. Moses got away and I got shot out of the air. A couple of the German aircraft were shooting at me as I floated down, that's where I got this damaged leg. I managed to walk and crawl to a wooded area. Luck was with me. There was a small cave there just large enough for me to crawl in. I stayed in it for three days. When I came out, I was so weak I could hardly stand but thank God rescue was still looking for me. I know this is a big order Sir but larger planes and something that can carry more fuel would help, in my opinion. We have top notch pilots in this unit, very good pilots. It just seems we are always getting into situations where we are outnumbered. I know we are short on air power at this time but if we had a few more planes, we could try to outnumber the Germans. It's hard to win when they have six to our two or twelve to our four."

"Thank you, Lieutenant Bear, you have just told me exactly what I needed to know."

McCloud put out the word that he wanted to see all the men in the squadron in the briefing room at 18:00 hrs. sharp. McCloud was a man who believed if you were going to do something get on with it.

In the briefing room McCloud said, "Good evening men, thank you for sharing your time off with me. As you no doubt know by now, I'm Major McCloud, your new Squadron Commander of the 207th Royal Fighter Squadron, or should I say what's left of it. That's what's brings us to this briefing room this evening. If we don't do something fast, we will soon be on our butts. This squadron has had a good name until now, so let's get to work and think of how to keep that good name, save our pilots' lives and airplanes. I'm open to any suggestions that anyone may have. I can use all the help that I can get, after all this isn't a one-man operation. It depends on all of us. I'll listen to all of your suggestions. I have been thinking, since we are short on planes and may not be able to get anymore very soon, that we might think about teaming up with the Americans and fly most of our missions in a formation type. I'm not prone to singling out names but, as Lieutenant Bear suggested, outnumber the Germans with air power. To do that we need to team with the Americans or the English, but I'd like to hear your opinion."

One man said, "I think that would be the thing to do, join the Americans. One reason, they have more planes than anyone else and seem to be able to get more just for the asking. Plus, the Americans seem to be the most aggressive ones here. I'd say go for it Commander."

McCloud asked, "What do the rest of you think about this type of move?"

He got an ok from most of the men present.

McCloud said, "Now there is one big thing some of you may not agree with, that is if we get the chance to join the Americans. Since they will have the most airplanes then they will most likely call most of the shots. For myself I don't have a problem with it. In fact, if it will save us from losing pilots and airplanes, I'm all for anyway they want to operate. Of course, we are just mulling this thing over at present."

McCloud said to Captain Albright, "Call headquarters and clear our squadron for a three day stand down. That will give me time to get in touch with the Americans and find out if this move we've discussed will suit them. If so, I'll talk to our headquarters commander and see if he will ok such a move.

The Major got the ok from the Wing Commander on joining forces with the American Fighter Squadron. Now he needed to discuss this deal with the Royal Air Force Headquarters. The next day he spoke with the Royal Air Force Commander, General Vernon York.

General York said, "I don't think I'm guessing when I say the Americans will be calling the shots, am I correct?"

McCloud said, "You are correct sir, but after all they will be providing twice as many planes as we do."

The American Squadron Commander, Colonel George Jones, called Major McCloud, and said, "I've run into a big problem concerning our joining forces on the flying missions, how are we going to get the word on the missions to each other without it getting into the wrong hands? If that should happen, we would be sending our pilots right into the German gun sights. Of course, telephoning is out. I had thought about a carrier, but on second thought that's no good either."

McCloud said, "This idea may not work at all and may not be ok by the top brass, but I'll run it by you and see what you think. How about when we are supposed to fly a mission, one of us moves our planes and pilots to yours or my base say a day before the mission, do our briefing and go from there, then try and get the next schedule date and the other squadron move to the other base."

Jones said, "It's worth a try, and you might think of putting together what we call an emergency aircraft parts kit. Of course, you can't carry enough to rebuild an aircraft, but you can save a lot of time with one. We have used them for years and they have saved us a bundle of time. Of course, all this depends on whether we get to go ahead on our plan or not."

At the first briefing, after the two squadrons got the go ahead on working together, Colonel Jones said, "Good morning gentlemen.

"I realize it's early but I'm sure you have heard that the early bird gets the worm. Well, I say the early airplane gets the German. Our assigned target today is big. It's spread out over several acres of land. It's a garment manufacturing plant. In fact, I think they make military uniforms. Two sections of this factory are underground. I'll take the section on the north, and you, McCloud, will take the one on the south side.

"One run is all any of you will make. If you think you have missed your target, don't try for a second run. Drop and get out. We depart here at 04:00, arrive on target at 05:12. You have been given a number. Use that number for your place in line. I'd like for you to drop at one minutes intervals. Any questions? Good let's fly, and good luck out there."

They arrived at the scheduled target with enough arsenal to destroy all of Germany. From the looks of things on the ground, as close as they dared to get before they started unloading on them, it looked like some of the facility was closed.

Jones said, "Men it appears we may not have had what we thought we had to drop on. Looks like some of it may have moved to another location. But stick to your places and proceed. See you at home. Good luck."

The factory building may not have been fully operational, but it was still heavily guarded. The twenty planes were being fired on way before they were ready to start dropping their weapons. Two American aircraft were hit very badly from ground fire and had to drop out of the formation. They learned later that neither one of them made it home. It wasn't clear whether the initial ground fire damage did them in or if they were fired upon after they broke formation and started home.

One pilot had reported he may have to leave the plane. He also said he had seen smoke from ground fire after they had turned back. The damage to his plane was in the fuel tanks. He ran out of fuel and had to bail out. It seems that the Germans picked him up.

Lieutenant Johnny McDougal was shot out of the air. No one saw a chute, so they didn't know if he bailed out or not. The remaining eighteen airplanes dropped their weapons and headed home as instructed.

At the debriefing Jones said, "Gentlemen, we must figure out a way to find and rescue Lieutenant Tommy Mammoth from the Germans. Captain Albright call rescue and see if they know anything yet about our downed pilots."

Jones called in McCloud. He said, "Major I understand that you were a prisoner of war in Germany not too long ago. Do you happen to know about where this prison was located? If so, check this map and show me where you think it was located."

McCloud looked at the map and said, "It is between here and here. That looks like about a ten-mile radius. Rescue can pin it down for you."

"We were thinking of that," said Jones, "But they are staying pretty busy. I was thinking of getting a Troop Carrier Squadron to drop a swat type team in there and rescue our pilots."

Rescue Commander Colonel Haskell P. Cummings, said, "We'll have to scout that prison a little before trying to take it over and rescue anyone. I'm sure since rescue made a good haul the other time, the Germans will be guarding this one pretty heavily. From what I hear the rescue swat team did a lot of damage to the other prison. It's hard to find men these days who will walk into a wall of bullets and do a job like that. To me they're hell on two legs.

"Anyway, give us a couple of days, maybe a week, to see what we can find out: how many guards, where they are stationed, what type weapons they have, who's in charge, and the lay of the land, Then I'll let you know if we can chance it.

If you get a bunch of men killed to save a dozen or so, then you haven't gained much, just kind of like a changeover of personnel."

The Canadians and Americans went on with their flying missions shooting up whatever they were assigned to, and of course getting shot at themselves.

MAJOR McCLOUD GETS AN UPGRADE

AFTER THE SQUADRON RETURNED from the day's mission without any mishaps, the orderly called the debriefing room and said that Major McCloud had an emergency call. He needed to come to the orderly room. The call was from General York, Royal Air Force Commander.

He said, "Major I'm at your base but I don't see any of our planes or personnel. Tell me, if you don't mind, what the Royal Canadian Air Force is doing on an American Air Force base."

McCloud said, "Yes Sir, I can explain that. Before I took command of the 207th they were losing two and three aircraft plus pilots, on just about every mission.

"I interviewed all the pilots and the majority of them said they believed the reason was because they went on their missions in small numbers. The German planes were bigger, faster and they could carry more than our planes. But by then since they'd lost several planes, they really didn't have enough to make a big show. So, we thought it over and came up with joining the Americans. With that many planes, maybe we would have a better chance of stopping this losing streak."

General York said, "I understand that but what I don't get is why are all of our planes and personnel on the American base?"

Major McCloud said, "That sir is for security reasons."

The General said, "Well, if you say so Colonel."

Major McCloud said, "That's Major McCloud Sir."

York said, "It's now Colonel McCloud. That is as soon as I can find you and pin the rank on you."

McCloud filled York in on the details of why they moved the aircraft and personnel to the American base.

York said, "That's why you're a colonel because you think ahead. That's what it takes in this war to stay ahead and alive. You'll be getting fifteen new aircraft with personnel to man them, and, of course, pilots to fly them. The first three or four will be delivered next week, and the remaining as the factory builds them. There will be two instructor pilots and two noncoms to train the ground personnel, also training personnel for the radio and avionics. Keep these people as long as you need them.

"Since some of your pilots think the Germans have bigger and faster planes than we do, they'll love it that this airplane is also bigger and faster and can carry more fuel than what you have now. So, it should fit the bill. Speaking of bill these planes cost a big bundle of money. They are made in America and the two instructor pilots are Americans."

McCloud called a meeting of all personnel.

He said, "Men, starting next week we are going to be very busy with three or four new and different airplanes coming in to replace the ones that we have now. I'll need some help and ideas on setting up a place to do our training on these new planes, something similar to what the Americans use, called FTD, Field Training Detachment. For that we will need a building with some type of seating like a classroom. I guess we could clean out the aircraft hangar but in a wide-open space like that and all the noise going on, it would be hard to concentrate. If the war hasn't destroyed everything, we might get the English to portion us off a classroom in the hanger. I'll see what I can do about it. They have their classroom in the hanger along with school room style desks, paper and pencils, and a little snack bar where one could get tea, coffee or soft drink."

Some of the men said, "See, all you have to do is ask."

"So, we will be shutting down our flying after the last mission Saturday. We will train until we are proficient with the new planes. I will also be asking you men for a lot of overtime."

They trained seven days a week for two weeks then backed off to six days a week after that. Colonel McCloud kept the training going and made sure everyone was getting what they were supposed to from the training. He was trying to make sure, which is very hard to do, that they didn't lose pilots and new planes right off the bat. It took a while, but they finally got all the planes.

Colonel McCloud said, "Men we are ready to go German hunting. I think we will surprise them with these new planes especially the speed and maneuverability of these magnificent airplanes. So be careful and be proud of the government for giving you such wonderful planes."

THE MISSION IS ON WITH NEW FASTER PLANES

AT THE BRIEFING COLONEL MCCLOUD SAID, "Men our target today is a factory that manufactures ammo and small weapons. If we hit the correct spot when the bomb explodes it should set off most of the ammo and it should destroy itself. We will depart here at 0410, arrive at drop zone at 0523. As before, drop and move out, no second pass over. If there is what intelligence says there is in that building when we hit the right spot it should create quite an explosion, a sight for sore eyes so to speak."

After the bombing run and on the way home someone said, "These new planes are great. Don't know how we got along without them."

At debriefing Colonel McCloud said, "Men, since we have these long-range planes, we'll go for two targets per mission. That will help get this war ended a little quicker and we can all go home. What do you think?"

Everyone said, "Let's do it!"

All the flying crews were down for one day to give the ground crews a chance to get the planes back in air ready condition. The next day they were back at it again.

At the briefing Colonel McCloud said, "We are scheduled for two targets today. The first one is an old airfield, not many planes on it, but we will try and get them and whatever else is sitting around. Do as much damage as you can to the runway. Rip it up so the Germans won't be able to use it. Then we go on to the second target which is a bridge and dam combination.

I'll give seven of you a number. The seven that get the numbers will hit the bridge, the rest will take the dam. We depart here in fifteen minutes, any questions? That's good."

OFF ON TIME AND McCLOUD IS HEADED FOR TROUBLE

THEY MESSED UP THE RUNWAY PRETTY GOOD then the bridge and dam. With the new planes Colonel McCloud didn't want to stop for the day. He had plenty of fuel and he wanted to use some more of it before going home.

He radioed the crew and said, "All you guys except Lieutenant Donald Church can go on home. I'll take Donald with me to look around at our next target for tomorrow. In the meantime, Captain Albright, you're in charge, out. Lieutenant, are you ready? Let's see how fast these new planes can really travel."

McCloud just had to show off the speed of the new planes. He was sure some of the Germans would be watching so they gave them a little of what they had. They went into Germany a little too far and got in trouble. The Germans had six faster more powerful planes to McCloud's two.

He said to Donald, "I'm not so sure we'll be able to fight our way out of this one, but let's give it a try. Give them everything you got left, then fire wall that thing and head for home base."

They still had plenty of ammo left but by that time the fuel was getting on the low side. They had enough to make it home but not enough to fight the enemy off for very long. About that time the German planes opened fire on them. The Germans were taking turns. McCloud knew they were really in trouble this time. He looked out and saw a wing of his plane all shot up and watched as it started to fold down. That's when he pulled the lever to eject himself. He could see the German planes shooting at him as he floated down to the ground. Then he saw Lieutenant Church's chute floating down. After they met they roamed around for several hours. Then McCloud finally found his pocket compass and got a bearing on the way home. It was a long walk but the Germans took care of that. They were picked up and taken in for interrogation and then to prison.

McCloud said to Donald, "This prison thing is getting to be old with me. General York is going to be disappointed in me for what I just led us into. The squadron is now short two planes and two pilots all due to my stupidity."

General York called Captain Albright and said, "What on God's earth was Colonel McCloud thinking about going off practically alone in enemy territory, sightseeing? He's been in a German prison camp before and was rescued. This time it may not be that easy, not to speak of costing the Canadian government the price of two new planes." He said, "Captain Albright you are now in charge until Colonel McCloud gets out of prison. Maybe longer, because if he does get out of prison, he may not be up to commanding a squadron of fighter planes. We'll just wait and see what happens.

BETTER FIND OUT WHAT JUNE IS UP TO

AFTER THE HOUSE CHORES WERE DONE June went to town to purchase a few food items. The storekeeper said, "June, that Mr. Henderson must think a lot of you and put a great deal of trust in you to leave his store account open to you. I've known him quite a long time and I didn't think he trusted anyone but himself, especially about his money. But he is a good and honest man. If I were you, I wouldn't let him get away."

June said, "Oh I'm just his housekeeper. I don't think he is interested in women. He has never said anything out of the way to me or tried to touch me. I have my own room. As I said I'm just his employee and friend nothing more. As far as I'm concerned, he is a gentleman."

The storekeeper said, "Well, what can I get for you today?"

This was a country store. People didn't ramble through the store fingering everything they saw and maybe sneaking a grape or two if no one is looking. The shopper told the storekeeper what they wanted, or do as June has done and give them a list of the items you wanted and the store keeper put the order together for you.

June gave him the list that she had written out.

She said, "I'll be back in about fifteen minutes. I'm going over to the bookstore. I need something to read."

She really didn't need a book because Mr. Henderson had a room full of very good books. She wanted to have a talk with the lady that worked at the bookstore. She wanted to see if she had any news that could benefit her. She didn't stay long because there was no news. June picked up her groceries and went home. She got supper started then sat down to rest and do some heavy thinking.

She said to herself, "I'm just not getting any place with this search for my half-brother. I just don't know what to do. I haven't saved enough money yet to hire a private detective. I'm sure they would require a retainer and that could be a hundred or more dollars. So, I'll just wait on that until I have the proper amount of money to pay for the search. To be truthful I really don't think a detective could do any more than I have since it's been a long time since Holstone disappeared. Honestly and truthfully, I don't think anyone can find him unless they knew him before.

"There's a reason behind him not trying to get in touch with some of his family, that is if he's still alive. The big thing is I haven't been able to figure it out just yet. I think what is driving me is that he's still alive somewhere and something mighty powerful is holding him back. I'm not getting any younger.

"Tom is another problem. It's good to know that I have another half-brother, but Mother dropped that one on me at the worst possible time. So, I'm just going to take them one at time. I don't even have a photo of Tom, but, on the other hand it would be so outdated it wouldn't be much help trying to identify him. All this work and no play is catching up with me. I'm well over twenty and haven't ever had a date. I mean a date with a real man. If I'm not careful, I'll be too old for that type of thing pretty soon."

On her day off she went home and cornered her sister Mildred.

She said, "Sis why don't you get involved in this half-brother search? You look for Tom, and I'll just stay where I am. To tell you the truth I'm just about exhausted and I've just about exhausted all avenues on this search. I think I'll slow down a bit."

Mildred asked, "How do I start and where, because I know nothing at all about this type of thing."

June said, "I didn't know anything about it when I started either. I'd check all the cemeteries in this area for names. I'd ask everyone in a certain age group if they've happened to see a young boy of Tom's age. I'd ask everyone I saw if they'd seen this kid. I'd check with the doctor. I'd go to the police station and find someone who worked for the police during the time that Tom was supposed to have left home. Mother said he may have been kidnapped by some coal miners/fishers while he was fishing with his brother.

"Remember someone somewhere knows something. The trick there is you must find that person, and, if you do, hope they'll open up and tell you what they know. The problem was I couldn't get anyone to talk. I could almost feel it that they knew something about him but weren't going to tell me anything. I thought at one time I had found a person that just might be our half-brother. But I checked him out the best I could. I work for him now and I don't think he is. But I'm not going to forget that he could be.

"I came across another man I thought could possibly be our half-brother. They both came to the town of Venus about the time our half-brothers disappeared, and they both came with nothing. One of them was Andrew Henderson, the other one is Nelson Phillips. I'm just not sure one way or another about them. I guess time will tell. When you get started on this search, that is if you will help out, come over and visit with me in Venus, and meet my boss. He is a real good person, and you just might pick up something that I've missed."

Mildred said, "I'll help out for a while on the hunt, and I'll come visit you one day next week, more than likely on Friday. Would that be ok with you?"

June said, "Friday is fine."

When Mildred saw Mr. Henderson, she almost lost her breath.

Later she said to June, "You had better go for that man because if you don't I will."

"Just a minute," June said, "I didn't invite you here to get involved with my employer. This isn't a match making game. Besides I may want him for myself. Later on, who knows what will come to pass. I'll introduce you to another man I've met and at one time thought he might be one of our half-brothers, but then I decided he wasn't. His name is Nelson Phillips, good looking man, well-dressed, very quiet, and stays to himself as far as I can find out."

After the introduction, Mr. Henderson said, "Mildred why don't you stay the night with us. We have plenty of bedrooms or you can bunk with June. You and June might want to go shopping tomorrow. That will give you both a little more time to catch up on your searching for your half-brothers."

She said, "That's mighty nice of you. I think I will stay because it's a long drive back home in the dark."

After supper June and Mildred went to June's room.

June said, "I do believe that man can read your mind. That's the second time he more or less told me what I intended to do next. Tomorrow when we go to town, I'll think of something to ask Nelson Phillips. That will give us the chance to go by his place. That is if he isn't at the restaurant. He stops by there sometimes for a cup of coffee. If we can find him, I'll ask him a few more questions about our half-brother. You can size him up and see what you think then later you can go see him and ask about Tom. From there you're on your own."

Mildred said, "I think I can handle it."

After breakfast the girls went to town, stopped by the restaurant, had a cup of coffee, and introduced Mildred to Mrs. May Lynn who ran the place. Then she asked if she had seen Mr. Phillips.

Mrs. Lynn said, "Yes he came in for breakfast this morning. He just left. Said he was going home so I guess you could find him there."

June said, "Thanks, I know where he lives. Let's go catch him before he leaves for his home in another town."

When they arrived and knocked on his door, he opened it and said, "Oh it's you June. Do come in."

June said, "Mr. Phillips this is my sister Mildred. "The reason we've come by is I had a couple more questions to ask you about my, our, missing half-brother. That is if you don't mind telling me."

He said, "I'll tell you anything to help if I know it."

June said, "My first question is approximately how old were you when Mr. Henderson arrived here?"

He said, "I was fifteen."

"Has Mr. Henderson changed since then, I mean in looks?"

"Well, to tell the truth, said Phillips, "He was so unkempt, and his cloths were in pretty bad shape, his hair was a bit unruly. Put all that together and it makes it hard to say who or what he looked like."

June said, "I understand."

He said, "I'm sorry but that's the best that I can do."

June said "That's ok. I guess we will see you again Mr. Phillips on the way back home."

After they left Phillips' home, Mildred said, "Well he isn't bad looking at all,'

June said, "Well now looks aren't everything but it's a good start."

Mildred said, "Well I've enjoyed the day with you June. It's time to start back to my home and do a heap of thinking about all we have talked about today and try to decide where to start if there is such a thing as a starting place in this situation. I mean Tom has been gone a long time and as far as I can find out there aren't any pictures or any type of papers on him, just the name Mother gave him."

On her way home Mildred realized she couldn't hold down a steady job and do very much searching for Tom. So, she decided to hire a detective to investigate this situation. If it became too expensive, she could always stop the search. The next week she got out the telephone directory and found a private detective, Herbert Carpenter. He told her what he charged per hour plus a retainer fee.

Carpenter said, "I'll need to meet with you and get some description of who you want me to find."

She said, "I'll come to your office. I'll be there in about twenty minutes."

Mildred gave the detective all the information she knew. She said, "He went missing before I was born. His name is Thomas Mansfield. He was twelve years old when he came up missing. Mother says that he and his brother were at the river fishing, and he could have been kidnapped at that time. His hair was blond. I know that's not much to go on but it's all that I have."

She had written down her address and phone number for detective. She handed him the paper and said, "I'll be in touch."

On her way home she said to herself, "I really think that was a waste of good money. I'll try him out for a couple of weeks and see what he is made of. I can always tell him to stop looking."

THE COLONEL AND LIEUTENANT IN TROUBLE

COLONEL MCCLOUD AND LIEUTENANT DONALD CHURCH found themselves in deep trouble. After they were interrogated, they were loaded in an open bed truck. The driver was driving faster than the old dirt road would bear and he seemed to be drinking. About two miles down the road the old truck got away from him and he left the road.

McCloud said to Church, "Jump."

They both left the truck before it hit a tree and caught on fire. McCloud pulled the driver out of the truck, but he was already dead.

He said, "May as well take his weapons. We might need them before we get out of this mess. I would take his uniform and dress up as a German, but I don't speak enough German to pull it off. How about you Church, do you speak any German?"

Church said, "Not enough to pull it off if we get caught."

McCloud said, "Come to think of it we will be out in the woods. The weather just might get cold. I see part of another uniform in the truck so may as well take all we can get. It's for sure we're not going to find a clothing store out here, plus I think I lost my wallet in the bail out or the interrogators took it."

So, they stripped the driver of his uniform and took the other clothes, weapons, some canned goods, and bread. By that time, the fire was getting hot, and the truck was just about ready to explode.

McCloud said. "Let's get into the woods because someone will be here shortly looking for the driver and of course us. With all that smoke the truck won't be hard to find. Let's make as few tracks as possible, make it as hard as we can for them to track us. I think I still have my pocket compass. I had it tucked away in my secret hiding place on my body. I'll take a reading as soon as we get over that hill. If I'm not mistaken England is that way."

They spent several nights in the wilderness. They saw several airplanes go over but they couldn't tell who they belonged to. The underbrush was so thick they could hardly see the sun. They couldn't tell which side was looking for them. After a few days the food they had taken was just about gone.

Colonel McCloud said, "We need to find a farm out here and see if we can get some food. It's too risky to shoot game for food because that will tell the Germans where we are if they happen to be close by."

In the distance they could see something that looked like a roof of a barn and house

McCloud said, "Let's head for that building that looks like a farmhouse."

It was almost dark when they reached the farmhouse and barn. They looked around and found some eggs and thank God, they found a room in the smoke house that had hams hanging in dozens, so they took one and hit the woods again. McCloud said. "I must have damaged my compass. It doesn't seem to be working, so we'll have to navigate by the sun and stars. They rambled around for two weeks finding very little to eat.

THE FARMER MUST HAVE TOLD ON THEM

THE FARMER MUST HAVE TOLD THE AUTHORITIES that he was missing a ham. He couldn't tell them that he had dozens of them else they would take them. The soldiers were tired, hungry, and plain worn out.

One morning McCloud and Church woke up looking at the muzzle of a gun in the hands of a German. He wasn't speaking English, but they knew what he meant.

Colonel McCloud said to Lieutenant Church, "I think we made a terrible mistake when we went back to the farm to get another ham. My compass was damaged somewhere along the line, and we wound up back at the barn. Since we were there, I thought we'd get another ham. But I think it got us caught."

The German said something and waved his rifle at them. They assumed that he said shut up and march. He marched them to a hut way out in the wilderness. He put them in a small room. Then another German came in. So far, they had only seen two Germans.

The one that had just come in said, "You," talking to McCloud, "Sit in that chair."

Everything around them including the building was shoddy. The floors were just dirt no wood. What the second German called a chair was also shoddily built. McCloud sat down.

The German walked back to what he called his desk and picked up a black leather bull whip.

He said, "I'm going to show you what we do to people that try to kill us with their bombs."

Church immediately saw the fire leap in the Colonel's eyes. McCloud hadn't told anyone about his childhood because it would break his word to Dr. Holt. When the German picked up the whip McCloud's childhood came flashing back to him.

He went berserk for a few minutes.

Church told later, "When the German struck Colonel McCloud with the whip fire in his eyes seem to leap out like daggers. I didn't know what was happening. Colonel McCloud sprang to his feet with lightning speed, grabbed the whip from the German's hand, rolled it around his neck twice and choked him to death.

"He grabbed his side arm and said, 'Get a weapon and let's get out of here.'

"By that time, the German that brought us in came through the door. McCloud shot him in the shoulder. He fell to the floor rolled around and held his shoulder trying to stop the blood flow."

Church said to himself, "I really can't believe my eyes. We have been in the wilderness for two weeks, tired, ragged, and nearly starved to death. But it didn't seem to hold the Colonel back. He seemed to have plenty of power. I don't believe there is anything that can stop him. I really think he could whip a dozen men."

The main prison seemed to be several hundred yards down a trail.

Church said, as he was running, "Colonel, Sir, let's go this way and maybe we can get back in the woods before the guards at the prison discover what has happened. They seem to be a little shorthanded on guards so I don't think the guards at the prison will leave their posts. They'll have to call in guards from somewhere else and that alone will give us time to be several miles down the way by the time that they get organized."

While he was running Church thought, "We could have used some of those canned goods that were stashed on the shelves back there but getting away was more important."

After they reached the tree line, they slowed down to a normal walk knowing that since they were near starved, they needed to conserve their strength and start looking for some food. McCloud wasn't saying much he was letting Church do most of the talking.

Church said, "There's a stream of water over there that may have some fish in it. It's mighty cold but I'm mighty hungry. I think I can walk up stream and sneak up on some of the fish and maybe catch enough for our supper. I found some matches in the coat pocket of the guard we pulled from the truck. On the other hand, I'm sure the Germans will be on our trail very soon and smoke from a fire would lead them straight to us but if I do catch some fish, we could dress them and lay them on a rock in the sun and dry the meat if we can wait that long.

"I'll pull off my boots and wade in the stream to see what I can catch for our supper. It's cold but we need something to eat."

He was in up to his knees when they heard someone coming through the woods.

McCloud said, "I'll hide until they pass us. You had better duck under that tree trunk over there on the other side. Maybe they'll get their water on this side of the stream and not see you. I'll take your boots with me but be careful, some of those guys can hear a heartbeat five hundred yards away, and you know water carries sound quite a way."

At those words the McCloud was gone, and Church was headed to the other side of the stream to get behind the trunk of a fallen tree. There were five Germans, all with weapons of course. McCloud could see them, but he was afraid to try and shoot them, afraid that he couldn't kill them all. Then the rest would know where he and the Lieutenant were.

He said to himself, "So much for that."

The Germans came up to the stream and filled their canteens, built a fire, and warmed up something over the fire. They made tea, talked for a while. After an hour they loaded up and left. They left the fire burning.

McCloud said to Church, "They left the fire going, so all we need now is the fish that you were going to catch. Since they left the fire going, we don't have to worry about them smelling the smoke of a fire."

Lieutenant Church went upstream looking for a fish he might sneak up on and have a feast here tonight. After about an hour and a half he came back carrying a fair string of fish. They wrapped the fish in some huge green leaves and baked them. It wasn't exactly a big fish fry, but it was food. After they ate the fish, they started looking around. They found a rifle leaning on a tree.

McCloud said, "Someone will be back for that weapon, and they will know someone has been here since they left. So, when he or they come we may as well kill them and get what food they are carrying, and if we're lucky maybe another weapon, or, we could move on and let them guess who was here after they left. I'll let you be the judge of that."

Church said, "If one or two come back we could do that, but if all five of them come back, then we could have a problem trying to get them all. Since we're outnumbered, I say put out the fire and go. Get as far as we can before dark catches us or the Germans catch us.

McCloud said, "Good thinking. You will make a great general one day."

So out went the fire and away they went hoping it was toward England. They left the rifle leaning up against the tree.

Church said, "Colonel, sir, those fish were very good. Where did you learn to cook like that?"

The Colonel said, "From camping and some of it just comes naturally for me I suppose."

The Lieutenant asked, "What did you season them with?"

The Colonel said, "A few herbs and wild onions."

They kept going until it became dark then looked for a place to rest for the night. They thought and hoped the Germans would be resting as well and not be looking for them.

All of a sudden, Church said, "I smell wood smoke and something cooking."

McCloud said, "Better look around and find out where the smoke is coming from. We are too far away from where we used the fire the Germans built, so it could be campers or could be a farmhouse out here or the patrol that we saw back there. Let's find out where that smoke is coming from."

When they found where the smoke was coming from, at first, they weren't sure because of the darkness, but then learned that it was four young German boys. So, they called out to the camp.

The boys said, "Come on in and sit with us. Have some of what we have to eat and drink. We haven't seen any humans out here in two weeks."

The Colonel said, "You've been here two weeks?"

One of the boys said, "Yes sir, let me introduce ourselves. I'm Antony, and Claus, Heinrich, and Wolfgang.

"We moved out here because of the war. We do not want to fight. If we didn't disappear they would have hanged us. Now I don't suppose we have a home to go back to, no jobs. So, we are on our own and just have to rough it. The food we're eating may not be suitable to you military folks, but it's all we have. So far it hasn't killed us, and you're welcome to part of what we have"

McCloud said, "We appreciate that and hope we don't get you into trouble. The Germans don't take to anyone aiding the enemy and they look upon us as their enemy of course."

Antony said, "Oh, they never come by here. They know we are four young boys and they got other things to do."

McCloud said, "We'll enjoy your company and food. We'll help you get more food for a few nights, then we'll move on. Don't want to be moochers and eat up all your food without helping replenish it. My friend, Donald, here is a fair fisherman. That is if you like fish."

Claus said, "We can't be choosy out here when it comes to food."

McCloud said, "We're trying to get back to our base of operations. A little bad luck hit us while we were flying, and we're being chased by the Germans. I don't think either one of us knows where the other is."

Anthony said, "I believe you folks are from, I'd say, Canada."

McCloud said, "Yes, we are here helping America and England with this war."

They teamed up and went hunting and fishing. McCloud thought it would be better to lay over there for a few days and try to fool the Germans. After three days they had caught fish, quail and a deer to pay the boys back for the food they had eaten. They left them plenty and took some for themselves. They said goodbye to the boys and went on their way.

MILDRED TAKES THE DETECTIVE OFF THE CASE

MILDRED CAME HOME FROM WORK and asked her mother if she had any phone calls.

Her mother said no, so she called her detective, Herbert Carpenter.

He said, "I have found one person that might have been your half-brother, but after further checking he turned out to not be who I thought he was. But I'll keep looking if you say so and if so, you owe me for another week's work."

Mildred said, "Let's hold on that for a while. I really don't make that kind of money."

He said, "I understand. If you should change your mind later, give me a call. Nice doing business with you. Sorry I couldn't come up with some good information."

Mildred went back to talk with Nelson Phillips, hoping he had thought of something more that he forgot to tell her.

After they had talked a while she said, "Mr. Phillips you have been very helpful to me. To show you how much I appreciate your help in this matter if you will accept, I'll treat you to dinner tonight. I know this is unusual but so be it."

He said, "Fine with me."

She said, "How about six p.m. at the Four Corners Mess Hall? The owner must have been a military person at one time."

After dinner he said, "Would you let me treat you to a movie since you have been nice enough to treat me to dinner?"

Mildred said, "I must get home tonight but how about tomorrow night? That's Saturday, there should be a new movie. Besides I think I've already seen the one that's playing now."

Mr. Phillips said, "O. K. We'll meet at the movie theater at six p.m., or let's make that five forty-five because the movie starts at six."

She said, "Fine by me."

On her way home she said to herself, "I sure hope I didn't mess that one up because he seems to be a very nice man."

She just had to go by and tell June about the excursion.

"I know my sister will be happy for me and shocked as well. But I must tell her before this gets any older. If I hurry, I may be able to tell her before Mr. Henderson arrives from work."

June said, "Well I'll be, and good for you." I hope things work out for you." Good men are few and far between especially in a small town like this. So don't keep him waiting."

After the movie Mildred and Mr. Phillips went for a walk around town.

Mr. Phillips said, "Mildred what brings you to town besides trying to find leads to your brother who's been missing for years."

She said, "Well it started out that way. But then-oh to be truthful with you-I was lonely and wanted to see you again. Is there anything wrong with that?"

He said, "Why no. I'm pleased that you did. If you hadn't come back, I would have come looking for you. I must say I'm pleased that we are open with each other. I think that's a good start. I've got things to do tomorrow but how about next Saturday. Would it be ok if I came to your home and picked you up?"

JUNE HASN'T GIVEN UP NOT BY A LONG SHOT

WHEN MR. HENDERSON ARRIVED AT HOME from work June had supper ready. He thanked the Lord for the food, the day, and their good life.

After they finished eating June said, "Mr. Henderson I haven't done any good trying to find my half-brother, at least the way I was going about it. So, what do you think about me writing a book using the real names of the missing, the family places, and time? I'll put all this in a book and try to get it distributed all over including the military. There is one big hold back, it's called funds."

Mr. Henderson said, "First of all call me Andrew, and second you write the book and take care of the distribution and I'll pay for it. If you want it to do the trick, make it free, that way folks will read it and it might get you some information."

June got busy writing.

She told Andrew, "I'm finding out real fast that I'm no good at writing a book, but in this case maybe it will get the message over to folks who will take the time to read it."

WHERE IN THE WORLD ARE YOU?

JUNE BEGAN BY SAYING, "My name is June Wonderland. I'm writing this book using the real names of the people that I mention in it. I'm trying to find my half-brother who went missing at a young age before I was born. His name is Holstone Wonderland. If he is living, he would be about thirty years old. Going by the looks of the rest of his family I'd say he would be a good-looking man as far as I can find out.

"He had no credentials when he left here. I think he would have blond hair, fair skin, blue eyes, 6'1", weighs about a hundred sixty pounds, and be easy going. Folks, this book is free to all who will accept it and read it. If you read this book and think you know where he is, please call me at this phone number or write to me at this address. Brother, if you happen to read this book and if you are free to talk about it, you will please many a heart by letting us know that you are alive and well. I have had the feeling ever since I found out about you that there is some sort of mystery involved in you being missing. If there is, and you feel that you can't talk about it for whatever reason, I will understand, and will not press the issue.

"Just let me know that you are still among the living. Please don't let the old hearts mourn for too much longer."

When the book was finished June had it published, and several thousand copies printed. She put in every library that she could get to, and put ads in papers, like Grit. She paid postage on all mailings of the book, she filled two rooms in the mansion with boxes of the book and just about ran herself ragged going to the post office to mail books.

The postman asked June, "What are you doing with all those books?"

She told him and gave him a copy.

Andrew arrived home from work and when he saw all those books, he said, "I see you have your work cut out for you. By the way, what is the title of your book?"

June said, "WHERE IN THE WORLD ARE YOU?"

He said, "That's fitting."

She said, "I don't really know how to thank you for this. I'm sure if I work for you a hundred years, I will never make enough money to repay you."

He said, "You can repay me by saying yes to the question that I'm going to ask you."

June said, "What would that be?"

He asked, "Will you marry me?"

She said, "Oh my goodness. I didn't expect this, I mean we haven't even kissed, held hands or anything in the line of a courtship. But of course, the answer is yes, yes, yes."

Andrew said, "I'm a man of few words. You set the date and invite your friends. I'll take care of the folks at the factory and here in town. You can list it in the local paper and announce it on the radio. As far as my friends outside of this town, I have none."

June said, "I'd like to set the date for June fifteenth."

Andrew said, "That's fine with me."

June excused herself and went to her room. She said to herself, "What in the world did I just agree to? Something I know nothing about. I don't know much about men. What am I supposed to do when we get married and start sleeping together? I've spent all my spare time trying to find my half-brother Holstone. I haven't had time for men or boys so I'm afraid I just overstepped my ability to carry this thing out. I feel like a kid at its first day in school. Maybe I should throw a few things in my suitcase, get in my car, and see just how many miles I can put behind me in what's left of this day."

So, after Andrew went to bed, she filled her suitcase, got what money she had saved, got in her car and hit the road. About three hours later she thought to herself. "This doesn't make sense I've never run from anything in my life. I've always met it head on. I mean after all I did say yes to Andrew, and he is a good man. I'd have to look far and wide to find someone his equal. He's been good to me and given me a job.

I'm sure he does love me, and he is very wealthy. So here I go back to Andrew and the mansion."

On the way back June thought her mother might enlighten her on what she needed to do on her wedding night. So, she headed to her mother's house. When she arrived at her mother's everyone was in bed.

Her mother said. "Do you know what time it is June? I mean I like to have you visit but there are daylight hours you know."

June said, "But mother I need to talk to you I need some information."

Her mother said, "Go on to bed and we will talk tomorrow."

June said, "No I need this information now. Andrew has asked me to marry him. I said yes. Now I'm not sure if I should have answered so quickly. What I need to know is when we are married what do I do. I know nothing at all about this type of thing. If I make a mistake, he will think that I'm a real dummy."

Her mother said, "Just act natural."

June said, "That's what I've doing all this time is acting natural and you see what it's got me into."

Her mother said, "June, I can't tell you what you should do. I mean every situation is different, every marriage is different. You can't just set a standard on something like this and say that's the way it's going to be done. It just doesn't work like that. As I said everyone is different simply because people are different. Dear child if you must talk about this thing tonight let's make a pot of coffee and I'll wake up and maybe tell you something that might help you get through the first night. It's been so long now for me that I'm not sure just what I did on my wedding night, probably acted like a real fool."

When they had mugs of coffee her mother said, "Now June, you just do what your body tells you to do. I'm sure Andrew will understand and help you get through this. I mean people get married every day and everything seems to turn out just fine for them and I'm sure it will for you so go on back home. Don't be a fool and lose this man. He's more than you will ever find anyplace else."

June said, "But mother, I've been so busy searching for Holstone I haven't even had a date with a man. Mr. Henderson is my employer and now he has asked me to marry him. We haven't even held hands, kissed, or really touched each other. I'm really his maid. I'm not sure I'm ready for married life. But I don't want to let this man get away. I want him for myself. I guess I'm afraid I'll mess up and he will get upset with me, annul the marriage, and send me home. I don't want that."

Her mother said, "As I said, just do as your body tells you to do. Act natural and Mr. Henderson will understand. Now get out of here and get back to him before he finds out that you are gone. "Get real, I mean grow up girl."

On her way home she was thinking to herself, "One thing for sure since Mr. Henderson has asked me to marry him that pretty well tells me that he isn't my half-brother. I mean if he was, I'm sure he wouldn't ask me to marry him knowing I'm his half-sister. So that pretty well settles that matter and I feel good knowing that."

At supper the next evening, June said, "Now that we're going to be married, would you mind telling me where you came from when you came here and started working for the boat building man?"

Andrew studied his plate of food for some time then raised his head and said, "It's best to let sleeping dogs lie. Ask me no questions and I'll tell you no lies. I will only say this which is not the answer you wanted of course, but life for me was hell and a struggle for years. Mr. Saddler was kind enough to give me a job which put food in my stomach, clothes on my back, and the will to press on. In my heart I shall never forget him. I'm renaming the boat factory in his honor. "It will be called The Saddler and his family will be taken care of as long as I live. End of conversation on this subject."

Andrew and June were married on June fifteenth. She had invited one hundred-fifty people; one hundred-twenty showed up. Mildred and Mr. Phillips were there and got to know each other much better. Andrew had closed the boat factory for two days and all the employees were at the wedding. Everyone had a very good time.

June said to Andrew, "Why don't we spend our honeymoon here at the mansion. It's so crowded in most towns anymore. We can read some books, have plenty of good food, and just relax."

Andrew said, "Fine with me."

The boat factory was renamed The Saddler. All the workers thought it was a nice thing to do. Five years went by rather quickly.

One day, Andrew was returning home from a business trip and was killed in a car accident. June closed the factory for a full week with full pay for all employees. She called Mr. Kindred and asked him if he would take the position of supervisor of the plant. He said he would. When she opened up the factory, she called a meeting of all employees. Some of them thought they would be looking for a job.

June told them, "There will no changes, except Joseph Kindred will be your supervisor. He knows the business and is willing to accept the job. I'll be in my office about two more days. Of course, I'll be in charge of the overall factory. My door will always be open to you. Any questions? Well good that must mean everyone is satisfied with the way things are going. Now let's build some boats."

Days, weeks, months and years passed. The boat sales were doing very well. In fact, they were so good, June announced a Christmas bonus for all employees and a five percent raise at the start of the new year. She expanded the factory to build a larger boat and hired twenty more people to build it.

June gave up the search for her brother. She thought it had been too long since it happened. She was sure the people who knew wouldn't tell anything about where her brother had gone.

June thought, "Well if he is still alive and wants us to know he will come to us. As for me, I'm closing the case. With the boat factory I've got just about all I can handle. We have a homecoming coming up this next year. Mother has asked me if I would make arrangements for it and do the invitations."

June invited about two hundred people.

She said to her sister, "I've got a lot of invitations to mail." She asked Mildred what she thought about having the home coming on the grounds of her mansion.

Mildred said, "I think that would be the best place since you have invited so many people. But I would have some Johnnies brought in because you don't want to have to clean up after that many people. Plus, you don't want them running loose in your house. You sure can't watch all of them all the time. I realize they are relatives, but they may bring a friend and you may not know the friend. In fact, when the people start coming in, I'd lock the doors and the gate around the courtyard and pool."

THE GERMANS HAD BEEN WATCHING THE YOUNG BOYS' CAMP

AS SOON AS THE COLONEL AND THE LIEUTENANT LEFT the camp, two Germans showed up carrying weapons.

One of them asked the boys if the fly boys had been there. The boys wouldn't answer them. The Germans wanted to know which way they went and what did they talk about. The boys still didn't answer them.

One of the Germans pointed his weapon at the younger and threatened him, but the boy still wouldn't talk. So, the German kicked him, knocked him down, then started kicking him in the face and stomping him.

The three other boys tried to stop the German. Shots were fired, one of the boys was killed, and another one was wounded.

Lester and Donald heard the shots and figured there was trouble at the young boys' camp.

Donald said, "I would bet that the Germans shot some or all the young boys. They will be on our trail soon, so why don't we find a good hiding place? When they come by, I'll get half of them and you the other half.

Lester said, "May as well, because if the Germans catch us again and we go to a prison camp, killing a few Germans is not going to make them hate us very much more than shooting and bombing the heck out of them."

Lester and Donald came to a place where they had to climb a steep hill. At the top of the hill was a large bolder and on the other side of the trail was a huge tree.

Donald said, "I'll take the tree and when the Germans climb the steep hill they will be out of breath. That will give us the advantage."

Lester said, "Good thinking, Donald."

Two hours later two Germans came down the trail. Lester and Donald let them get about two thirds way up the hill. Their huffing was getting louder.

Lester whispered, "It's time to let them have it."

After they shot the soldiers, Lester said, "We had better get moving, leave this trail and get into a place where it's hard to track us. The Germans will be wondering why those soldiers haven't returned to base. They'll start looking for them and when the bodies are discovered, the force will be after us."

They left the trail and walked until nighttime was moving in.

Lester said, "We had better find us a place to, hopefully, get a bit of rest before the Germans come moving in."

Lester and Donald woke up looking down the barrel of a what looked like a cannon, but it was a much smaller weapon than that, something like a thirty-caliber weapon. This time there were just too many Germans for Lester and Donald to think about overpowering them. One of the German soldiers spoke perfect English.

He said, "On your feet you murdering rats. There is going to be a long walk ahead of you and if you try any funny moves with me, I'll shorten that walk."

They walked for two days and were worn out when they saw something that looked like a prison.

Donald said, "I hate to say such a thing but I'm glad to see that prison, that is if it is a prison. I don't have any feeling left in my feet. They hurt until they went numb several miles back."

They didn't get anything to eat that night. Early next morning they were taken to a small room near a tower where guards with machine guns were normally located. But Lester, always on the lookout for these things, saw there was only one guard in the tower and no one on the ground. The guard in the tower was armed with a small caliber rifle, not a machine gun. These things are important when you're trying to escape. They were both questioned as to what they were doing out there rambling around and killing German soldiers.

Lester replied, "The Germans were trying to kill us, so it seemed like the thing to do at the time. That's the name of the game, save thy butt by all means."

The interrogator said, "Don't get smart."

Lester said, "If I'm not mistaken your country started this war."

The interrogator slapped Lester across the face with his leather gloves and replied, "Any more of that talk and I shall get tough with you."

Lester said to himself, "I'll even that up with you if I get the chance. Like every dog has its day."

The interrogator turned to Donald, but he didn't have much to say. He answered as little as possible.

The interrogator said, "I'm a bit short handed around here so I'm going to put you guys to work. Don't expect any favors just because you are helping build a German prison camp. Remember you will be watched at all times and that soldier in the tower will shoot to kill.

"The tools and items that you will need to do the job are over there in that little building. Your first job will be to dig holes six feet deep. and four feet wide then build a building over each hole. I'll need four of them. In case you don't know they are called privies."

Lester and Donald went to the little building and selected a dirt pick and shovel.

Lester said, "I don't think there are any bugging devices in this dump, so I'll say this to you. If there are only two of us and two of the Germans, we have an excellent chance to escape this place tonight. Of course, they'll be thinking the same thing. But if they don't bring in more guards, with just the two of them they have to sleep some time. When they go to sleep that's when we make our move. I think it's going to be very easy because they are not very well organized. As you can see, this prison, if you can call it a prison, has just opened. I'm guessing that we're the first prisoners to be assigned here. So, let's be mister nice guys until we get our break."

That break came about three in the morning. Lester walked into the guard house, picked up his and Donald's weapons, and put a rope around the interrogator's neck. He tied it so tight that the interrogator stopped breathing, while Donald was sneaking up on the supposed guard. Donald couldn't find a rope, so he used wire which served the purpose very well. He picked up their weapons and some canned food items.

Lester said, "We're in this pretty deep so we may as well take this old truck and ride it until it runs out of petrol. I'm guessing that we have about two-and-a-half hours before light. Then we need to go into hiding again."

They ran the truck until they thought it was just about out of gas and just so happened, they were near a river and the light of day was upon them. So, they ran the truck into the river and watched it sink out of sight.

Donald said, "Now if a good rain will come and wash away the tire marks, the Germans will have a difficult time finding the vehicle. They will think we are still driving it, which will give us a little time."

They started walking again in the direction they thought was toward their base. But in a strange land who can be sure?

Lester said, "Well it's not like the comforts of home, but we're still alive and free. I guess you could call it free since we're not in a German prison. I'm wondering how Captain Albright is doing as commander. Those airplanes we heard overhead sounded like ours. I was wondering if it was him, if so, I have no doubt that he was looking down at the ground every chance he got looking for us."

CAPTAIN ALBRIGHT TAKES UP THE SLACK

CAPTAIN ALBRIGHT SAID, "Men we must figure out a way to locate Lester and Donald. I'm calling him Lester because he asked me to, especially in a case like this, and Donald, I'm sure, would go along with it. So, until further notice it's Lester and Donald. So, I'm trying to figure out a way to locate them unless the Germans have already done so.

"Nevertheless, the mission for tomorrow will be a small airfield. I believe most of it is being used as a stockpile of ammo and spare parts for airplanes, tanks, guns, personnel belongings like uniforms, rifles, and what the Americans call C rations.

"So, let's see how much damage we can do to it. As before one pass and leave because we don't know for sure how much security there will be at four in the morning, yes, four in the morning. That's our target time. We brief at two-thirty, break ground at three-ten, hit the target at four. All good round numbers don't you think?"

All he heard was groans.

The day went well until they neared the target and found out very fast that there were functional German aircraft on the base ready to hit the air after them.

Captain Albright said, "Well looks like we run for cover if there is any cover. So, let's head for those clouds and just maybe they will cover us long enough to get away."

All twelve planes headed for the big sky and big fluffy clouds. The clouds did help but they were a long way away from home base and the cloud formations didn't last all the way home. Six German planes caught up with them and shot two of the Canadian planes down at that point. Then here came

117

the Americans with, it looked like, enough fire power to wipe out the universe. That was a delightful sight to see, twenty planes loaded for bear. The Germans didn't want anything to do with that many experienced pilots, so they turned back but not in time. The Americans gave chase and shot all six of the German planes out of the air.

One of the Canadian pilots said, "Those Yanks are hell in the air. Sure, glad they were here today."

The captain asked, "Did anyone see Brad's and Jeff's chutes?"

One of the men replied, "We were so busy getting shot at I don't think anyone had a chance to look."

Captain said, "I'll ask the Americans if they saw any chutes going down. I need to thank them anyway for helping out.

"Calling the American fighter pilot leader come in please."

The voice said, "This is the leader. What can I do for you today?"

Captain Albright said, "This is the Canadian pilot leader. You have already done it. Thanks a million. Did you happen to see any chutes floating down from our two lost planes?"

The American pilot said, "Negative. Is there anything else that we can help you with today?"

Captain Albright, "No thanks, just come over and visit with us sometime when you're not shooting down Germans. You could no doubt teach us a thing or two about air combat.

"Well crew, it appears we may have lost two good pilots. It saddens me to have to say that."

He said, "Let's go home, I've got work to do."

Captain Albright called General York and said, "General, sir, we have apparently lost two more pilots."

General York asked, "How did it happen?"

Captain Albright said, "The only thing I figure is that they were waiting for us. They had us outnumbered again just like before. We need backing from other sources of planes. We are going in with almost a skeleton crew, if you will, and the Germans are coming at us with double that. If we can't get more planes and pilots so we can at least match their numbers, then we need to team with the Americans and English to try and match the Germans that way."

General York said, "Good thinking, Captain. I'll see what I can do and be back with you on the results tomorrow morning."

Captain Albright said. "We have a mission early tomorrow morning but will return around eight ten hundred."

The next morning was more or less the same as the other missions except after the bombing raid the captain was wondering where the German planes were. They bombed the aircraft factory and didn't see a German plane.

The captain said, "Let's go home."

As they approached the base, they knew right off that something was very wrong. The base was covered with fire and smoke, there wasn't a runway left to land on.

The captain radioed the American base and said, "This is the fighter pilot leader of the Canadian Air Force. We don't have a base left to land on. Do you have room for us?"

The American Colonel said, "We'll make room. Just give us fifteen minutes to clear a few items out of the way."

THE ROYAL CANADIAN AIR FORCE JOINS FORCES WITH THE AMERICANS AFTER THEIR BASE IS DESTROYED

COLONEL JONES, AMERICAN FIGHTER SQUADRON commander, called General George Flatt, American fighter wing commander.

The first thing the General said was, "Colonel what's going on down there?"

Jones replied, "Well, Sir, it seems that while the Royal Canadian Air Force, led by Captain Albright, was on mission with, I believe, four planes, the German Air Force hit the base and from what I understand wiped out the entire force of planes that were left on the ground and, I assume, all personnel and equipment. Captain Albright, acting commander of the Royal Air Force Fighter Squadron, radioed me when he returned from a mission and saw what the Germans had done to their base. He said they needed a place to land their planes and regroup and I told him come on in. He is here with what is left of their pilots and planes of the 322 Royal Canadian Air Force. He is very upset over all this, but I'm sure he will have a full report ready very soon for General York, the Royal Air Force Commander."

Flatt said, "I'll be down in about two hours. I want to get together with General York. We need to change our strategy. So, if General York arrives before I do, set up an appointment for me with him. It's very important."

Jones replied, "Consider it done sir."

General York arrived fuming, not at the pilots, but at the Germans.

He said, "Captain Albright, give me a complete detailed report on this situation. I need to know all details when I make my report to home base in Canada. Don't get me wrong, Captain, I'm not blaming you for this and I do understand. But those at home may not. While you're at it, you might give some thought on which way you want to go since you only have four planes left. You may be forced to join the 307 Royal Canadian Air Force. I know before you lost most of your planes there wasn't room there for two squadrons. Then again home base may pull you out of the war. Of course, I'll do everything I can to hold onto both squadrons but sometimes my grip on things gives up and I have to let go."

Albright said, "Well, sir I think the Germans really meant to destroy everything on the base. They just got there a little late. They didn't expect us to be on a mission at one thirty in the morning, otherwise you wouldn't be talking to me. I think the reason we were losing planes on missions was simply because we were outnumbered by the Germans. You simply can't compete with four against ten and twelve planes. The odds are just too great.

"I really don't know how to start notifying the families of all the Airmen who were assigned to the base. I'm waiting now for a report from Chaplain David Horthorne and Captain Charles Hatfield on what they found on their inspection of the damage done to the base. They may find someone alive, but I seriously doubt it. Along with that I'll try to find the emergency data on all personnel listing names and addresses of their homes. But all of that information may have been destroyed in the bombing. If that fails, I'll have to get it from headquarters back home and that could take a little time. So, if it's ok with you, I'm holding the squadron on the ground for a little while.

The General replied, "You do as you see fit and I'll back you."

GATHERING OF THE GENERALS

GENERAL YORK, GENERAL FLATT and General David Mathew arrived at the base. General York asked Colonel Jones, the squadron commander, where they could hold their meeting so that they would not be disturbed and that no one could overhear what was discussed.

York said, "Colonel I want you there as well. You need to know what the plan will be as well as we do. It could very well mean more work for you and your pilots."

Flatt opened the discussion by saying, "Well gentlemen looks like we're all here, so I'll get on with what I have to say."

Jones said, "Pardon me General for breaking in but this news may be pertinent to this whole discussion."

Flatt said, "Very well Colonel. Let's have it."

Jones said, "Just before coming in this room, Captain Hatfield told me part of what they found at the base that was bombed by the Germans."

Flatt asked, "Where is this captain now?"

Jones replied, "He and the chaplain are waiting outside."

Flatt said, "By all means bring them in. I want to hear all of what they found."

Jones brought the chaplain and Hatfield in and introduced them to everyone in the room.

He said, "Captain tell the group what you and the chaplain found on your inspection of the base the Germans hit."

Captain Hatfield replied, "There wasn't much left that they didn't hit. It appears that they made several bombing runs over the base and runway. It appears that they left most of it in ruins. As a matter of fact, I didn't find anything that hadn't been damaged and some of it is still burning. This part I wish I didn't have to say but may as well. I'm quite sure there aren't any survivors. Some of the dead will be hard to identify."

Flatt said, "Captain what are your thoughts. Is it feasible to rebuild the base?"

Hatfield replied, "Sir, in my opinion, it would cost too much and take too long. I think we should level it and put a marker up and take our planes elsewhere."

Jones said, "We'll make room for the four planes and crews if you want to join us. General, sir, what do you think?"

He said, "Some of the crews may have to be housed in tents until we can get the ok on building more barracks, but other than that, I see no other problems."

York said, "Now that we have that problem solved, we must come up with a change in the way you have been scheduling your missions. We have lost too many pilots and planes. If anyone has an idea on what we need to do. I'm here to listen."

Mathew said, "I suggest using more planes on the missions. It will cost more of course but it might save the lives of our pilots and, if possible, when possible, join forces with the 307 Royal Canadian Air Force fighters. When the Germans see that many airplanes coming at them at the same time, they'll think again about sneaking up on a sleeping base of personnel. Do I hear a second to that idea?"

General Flatt replied, "I do have one thought on that suggestion. What if the Germans get word of this set up and assemble everything they have in the local area and wipe us out? I mean, everything that we have put up there. If that little scenario should happen then, gentlemen, we have no way of defending ourselves. That would let the Germans finish us as they please. I realize that is not very likely to happen, but, in a war like this, anything is possible. On the other hand, I agree with General Matthew. Now does anyone have a better idea?"

Jones said, "I agree with General Matthew. Another thing I've been thinking about since the Germans attacked after our mission planes were launched and bombed our base, they won't forget how easy it was to destroy a base and get away with it. So, what I'm saying is they are likely to try the same thing on other bases. We need to get a better early warning system set up and now before anything like this happens here."

Flatt said, "I'll get headquarters on that tomorrow, and I'll have more anti-aircraft guns stationed at all our bases. I'm sure there are guns sitting in some warehouse rusting. So, I'll have them put to good use."

Albright said, "I appreciate this from you Americans, but it won't be of much help with just four planes left in my squadron. General York, sir, are there plans to rebuild the 322nd with planes?"

York said, "As of now the answer is no but as you know things change. Of course, this will be up to the home base personnel to make that decision. Don't lose any more planes or you may be out of a job. So, we will go at the Germans full force is that correct?"

Everyone said they would give it a try.

York said, "If the mission problem is settled, we need to get rescue involved in searching for Colonel McCloud and Lieutenant Church. "They have been missing three months now. They could be in a secret prison, dead, or half starved to death out there, but we need to know more than missing in action. Captain Hatfield you would be a good man for that job if it's o.k. with General Flatt. I hope I didn't overstep my bounds by suggesting something that's none of my business since you are an American."

Flatt said, "How about it Captain?"

Hatfield replied. "I don't know much about that type of operation, but I'll give it a try. I'll need three or four crewmen."

Flatt said, "What about it General York? McCloud and Church are your men. I'm furnishing the leader; can you furnish the crewmen?"

York said, "Of course, When do you want to start Captain?"

Hatfield said, "Since this is Friday, I'd like to start Sunday morning. Going on a Sunday morning might keep us out of sight for a while."

York said to Albright, "Do you have a couple of men that you can give up for a good purpose?"

Albright said, "I'll have them report to Captain Hatfield Sunday morning."

LESTER AND DONALD ARE STILL MISSING

LESTER SAID, "Donald at the rate we are going the war will be over before we are found."

Donald said, "If so, I sure hope they don't give up on us."

Lester said, "Well the war is still going on because I see and hear our planes flying over. I've been trying to get a course on where they are coming from. That would help us find our base, which may still be a long, long way especially since we are on foot. I can also hear bombs and gun fire which tells me we are still close to where the Germans are based.

"Our best bet is to watch for our planes. Depending on the time they come over we will know they are on their way home if it's, say, five-thirty or so, if they are still scheduling missions early in the morning, also if their flight path to the target puts them over us. Of course, there will be other targets that will take the planes in other directions. Oh well, we'll just do the best that we can. But without food I'm getting pretty weak and I'm sure you are too.

CHANGING THE WAY THE MISSIONS ARE SCHEDULED

GENERAL FLATT SAID TO THE GROUP, "I want a meeting with all American and Canadian pilots. Have them in the briefing room at 18:00 hours, that, of course, is with all personnel that are in this room at 18:00 hours."

Flatt asked, "Are all personnel present?"

Colonel Jones replied, "All present and accounted for sir.

Flatt said, "Gentlemen, listen up and take notes if you like. We are changing the way you are scheduling and flying these missions. The Germans are on to the time that you are taking off from the base and they are ready for you. This is going to change right now. The next mission will be Monday morning. Launch time will be 08:12. Half of the planes will come in on the target from the west at tree top level and, of course, max speed. The other half will come in from the east at twenty-one thousand feet. The antiaircraft gunners will see or get word of the planes coming in at treetop. Their guns will be on the low fliers. While that's going on, the other half at twenty-one thousand feet will start their dive and should be able to put the bombs right in the Germans' watch pocket. I realize you've been heading home after only one pass but, if this works, the half of the squadron that made the dive head home in case the Germans are aware that we have left the base unguarded and the half that was flying low can make a second pass over the target, providing you have weapons left. The Germans, what's left of them, will wonder where in heck all those planes came from. Of course, if this works you can only use it a couple of times then change to a new tactic, because the Germans will be looking for it to happen again. So, use it a couple of times and think up different ways to hit them then later go back to this tactic again. That will keep them on their toes.

THE PILOTS WERE PLEASED FOR THE CHANCE TO SLEEP A LITTLE LONGER

BRIEFING AT 07:30 HRS. WENT WELL. Most of the pilots were wide awake.

Colonel Jones said, "Gentlemen, as the General said yesterday, launch time is 08:12. Flying time to target is fifty-eight minutes. The numbers I have given out, one thru twenty, the first ten numbers will be the planes to fly at tree top level and at max speed. The second ten numbers will fly at twenty-one thousand feet then dive on the target thirty seconds after the low fliers have cleared the target area is that clear? Timing here is essential. Time hack your watches. I don't want any mistakes here like flying into each other. The weather is clear out there today, so you shouldn't have any trouble seeing what's going on. After you've dived and released your bombs you are to head home to defend this base as directed by General Flatt. The low-level fliers can make a second pass over the target providing you have enough bombs and, of course, fuel, which shouldn't be a problem. Good luck men."

Just then General Flatt stepped in and said, "Be careful out there gentlemen. I'll be waiting for your return and your debriefing. Wish I was going with you. Have fun and God be with you.

All twenty airplanes returned safely to base.

At the debriefing, General Flatt wanted to know how things went and what the pilots thought about the changes. Everyone seemed to be well pleased with the changes.

Colonel Jones said, "General, I do believe the way you set this new scheduling up really caught the Germans off guard.

When they saw the low-level fliers coming in at tree top level, they thought that was it and probably didn't see or hear the second wave of planes coming in from up above. But I'm sure we destroyed that battery. Thanks General, Sir, I think you have saved the day."

General Flatt said "I'll be letting you know about the early warning system I'm going to try to get set up here. You, Colonel, can be working on the alert standby aircraft and personnel. Just a few pointers on that. I want the crews that are on alert duty standby in the seat of the plane and the crew chiefs and maintenance personnel in a vehicle alongside the plane. That's two planes. Make that two hour shifts per crew then change and that's also twenty-four hours a day, seven days a week. Because if you pilots are in the rack sound asleep when an early alert whistle blows, by the time you get to your plane, you may not have a plane."

Colonel Jones said. "You heard what the General said. That's the way it's going to be."

Colonel Jones asked General York, "Sir, are the maintenance and crew chiefs that were lost in the disaster at the Canadian base going to be replaced? The addition of your four planes has put a little more of a workload on my personnel. Don't get me wrong. I'm pleased to have them here and working with us, but a little more help in the maintenance area would be very welcome."

General York said, "Oh yes, as matter of fact, there are some on the way. I have specialists from all fields, plus crew chiefs, and I ordered twelve airplanes. Of course, the planes will come as soon as they are built. Also, there will be pilots sent here to fly them."

Colonel Jones said, "If you want to have the parking area enlarged and of course billeting for personnel, I think this would be the best place for your squadron to operate from. We could work closely together on our missions. In fact, that would be a great help to me to have them close by. Because no doubt in the future we will have grounding condensation on some of planes and from time-to-time ten percent of our planes are out of commission for one thing or another. When that happens, your squadron can fill in the voids."

General York said, "Colonel that's good thinking. I'll see what I can do."

GENERAL FLATT RETURNS WITH GOOD NEWS

GENERAL FLATT RETURNED AND ANNOUNCED that the early warning system would be updated starting Monday morning. He asked how the standby alert was going.

Colonel Jones said, "A few complaints, but overall, I think it will be worth the effort. The crews will get used to it and take it as just part of the job. I mean they realize as well as I do that this war is no picnic. Some people would complain if hung with a new rope. But they are a good bunch of men.

"General, Sir, I think I'll use the same scheduling system we used on the last mission. I'll use it one more time then come up with another way to attack the Germans on the next mission."

General Flatt said, "That's fine. Don't overdo it with any one system. Just a suggestion, you might think of staggering the planes. Say if you have twenty planes on the next mission, put five in the air at a time, and the next five three minutes apart and if possible, hit the target from different directions with each five planes. Have each set of five fly at different altitudes. Just little things like that make a difference sometimes."

IT APPEARS THE GERMAN SPIES WERE DOING THEIR JOB WELL

ON WEDNESDAY, GENERAL FLATT ANNOUNCED that the modification of the early warning system would start on the coming Monday. The work crews had been set up and supplies ordered, but somehow the Germans must have got wind of what was going on. So, they hit early, 02:21 a.m. The old alert system sounded, but too late to save anything. No one had time to count the planes, but they knew that there were in the neighborhood of at least thirty plus. They hit so swiftly that no one had time to get to the airfield and into a plane before the Germans' bombs and gunfire were all over the base. Of the sixteen airplanes the Americans had there and four of the Royal Canadian Air Force, when the Germans were satisfied, and headed home, there were eight airplanes left. Unknown to the others, two American pilots did make it off in time to get into a shooting battle with the Germans and put one of the Germans' planes out of their inventory. But after the Germans realized what had happened, they ganged up on the American pilots and destroyed both of them. Since there was so much going on no one saw a chute so they didn't know if the two pilots made it out of their planes or not.

Colonel Jones said, "Well gentlemen we have work to do. First of all, check the planes that we think weren't damaged and make sure that they are flyable. You, Lieutenant Muluks, check the sleeping quarters, the orderly room and all other buildings, any place that personnel were when the Germans hit and give me check on the casualties."

Lieutenant Muluks returned in two hours with bad news. He told the Colonel that every building on the base was damaged, some more than others.

"Casualties are high. I counted twenty-two but we need to dig through the rubble. When we do, I'm sure there will be others. The men that I found alive I put to work looking for wounded or dead. I told them to report to you or me as soon as they finished. They are also to salvage all goods that they find that are still serviceable, like clothing and food, and put them where they would stay dry, that was if they could find a building that was still standing and had a roof on it. Because the weather forecast is calling for heavy rain tonight and tomorrow."

THE TWO PILOTS THAT WERE SHOT DOWN DID BAIL OUT

BEAVER AND CHUCK WERE IN PRETTY GOOD SHAPE after they landed. They knew the Germans would soon be looking for them, so they started looking for a place to hide themselves and rest for a couple of hours. They hadn't been asleep but for a couple of hours when they heard something coming down the trail.

Beaver said, "Let them pass. Then we'll come up behind them and hit them over the head with our walking canes and get their weapons."

The two young Germans, more like boys, walked right past Beaver and Chuck without seeing them. They seemed to be busy chatting about something they were going to do when their shift was over. Beaver and Chuck let them get about a hundred yards up the trail. Beaver was light footed. He could sneak up on most anything. He hit one of the men over the head and while he was falling, Chuck was beating on the other one grabbing the German's rifle.

Beaver said, "It's sad to shoot a man with his own weapon, but if we don't shoot them, they will tell on us or be on us until they kill us.

Chuck said, "You know, since these men are about our size, we could take their uniforms. They might come in handy on down the road. If we put them on it might get us a little time if we run into more Germans."

Beaver said, "It's late and dark is coming on, I'm wore out and this looks like as good a place as any to spend the night."

Early next morning they heard footsteps coming down the trail.

Chuck said in a low voice, "It's two Canadians."

As they walked past Chuck said, "Hey you, where do you think you are going?"

He forgot he was dressed in a German uniform.

Lester said, "Oh no, two Germans!"

Beaver walked out and said, "It's ok. We're Americans."

Then he said, "My God, you're the commander who's been missing for several weeks. Forgive me, Sir, for speaking to you in that way."

Lester said, "It's no problem. Just pleased to see some of our own. But I would like to hear about the German uniforms."

Beaver seemed to be the spokesman for the two. He said, "We had to kill two Germans who were looking for us, and, since they were about our size, we decided to take the uniforms. Can't tell, they could come in handy, or they could get a person killed when they stopped for the night."

Lester was thinking, then he said, "I don't want you men to think that I'm taking over when I say this. If either one of you men want to do the planning, then that will be fine with me and if not, I'll be glad to do the planning."

Everyone said, "Fine with me Colonel."

He said, "Well, I've been thinking, and, if I'm not mistaken, there is a prison about ten miles up this river at the bend of the river, and just a few yards from where a smaller river joins the larger. I've seen it when we flew this way on missions, and, if I'm correct and you men agree, when we find it, you, Beaver and Chuck, with the German uniforms can pretend to be bringing Donald and me in as your prisoners. From there we'll release the prisoners. I'm sure there are several of our troops in there."

Everyone said, "Fine with me."

Lester said, "Then I'll work out the plan of attack."

After they had walked for what seemed to be thirty miles, Lester said, "There it is way up there by the river's bend." He said, "Donald, you go as close as you dare to the prison and find out what you can find out about personnel, location of all buildings, number of men on the gate and tower, number on guard of the officer in charge of dogs, and whatever else that you think we might need to know."

Donald returned with news.

He said, "Two on the gate, two in the tower, one guarding the officers building, two in the kitchen, about twenty prisoners working with two guards. All Germans have weapons."

Lester said, "OK, this is the plan. Just as dark is falling, Donald and I will hand over our weapons to you, Beaver and Chuck. You march us up to the gate say as little as possible. I'm sure the guards will motion you toward the officers' hut. As the door to the hut is opened, Beaver and Chuck will pass the weapons to me and Donald. I'll shoot the officer and guard; Donald will get the two on the tower. Beaver gets the gate guards. Chuck, you get the two cooks, and we'll go from there on anyone else that might be hanging around.

"After we are sure there aren't any more Germans, we start looking for our prisoners. Assemble them in the middle of the grounds. Find some type of transportation, anything that has wheels and will run, load the prisoners and move. There must be trucks sitting around. When you're rounding up the prisoners, some of them may not be able to think for themselves and may need to be carried. That depends on how badly they have been treated here. Do not, I repeat, do not leave anyone behind."

As Chuck came from the mess hall, he was carrying two large boxes.

Lester said, "What in the world do you have there?"

Chuck said, "We need food, and I found some cheese and bread and several other things in the mess hall. I thought we could no doubt use them since we haven't had a decent meal in several days."

They rounded up the prisoners and got a head count of 50 men.

Lester said, "We need at least three trucks, but take four if we can find them."

Chuck said, "Colonel, while I was in the mess hall, I saw several cans of what I'm sure is gasoline. We may need it before we find our base."

Lester said, "Load it up and everything you see that you think we might use."

Two of the prisoners got hit by stray bullets, but none of the wounds were serious. One of the prisoners was a medic and he took care of the gunshot wounds with what was available.

Lester said, "Let's go men. The enemy will be on us shortly. Donald, take the smaller truck and make a last check of the buildings in case we have overlooked someone. In the meantime, the rest of you start moving these prisoners. We need to put some distance between us and the Germans. We are not sure where we are and where our base is, so we'll just go north for a while."

After they had climbed a steep hill, one of the prisoners said, "Colonel, I see dust rolling up from that field we just passed about two miles back. I'm guessing it's Germans trying to catch up with us."

Lester said, "Well we have several weapons and several cases of ammo that we picked up at the prison after the shooting, so I think we can stand them off for a little while anyway how many vehicles do you see?"

"I'm not real sure due to the dust but I think there are four trucks."

Lester said, "We might be able to use the trucks, so let's dig in here and set ourselves up to wipe them out. They won't be expecting us to be ready for them, so we'll give them a little of our well thought out advice. When they show up, they'll be slowing down coming up that grade. When they reach the point where that old dead tree stump is, that's when we will let them have it."

The Germans pulled a little sneaky trick on them. Some of them went on foot at the bottom of the hill, went around to the north side, sneaked up on Lester and his group. They shot and killed six of the prisoners, but Donald and Beaver took care of the shooters.

Lester said, "Well, we don't know how many more days or even weeks we will be looking for our base and hoping for a rescue, so we may as well bury our dead here. I'm not too concerned about the Germans but, if anyone wants to do the duty of burying them go ahead. I think we killed 12 men. All I want from them is their vehicles, food for the prisoners, and weapons. Pretty soon we'll have enough weapons to give one to each of the prisoners. I think we'll bivouac here, get the prisoners fed, and a good night's sleep. We'll see what's in store for tomorrow."

Early next morning they heard the noise of low flying aircraft.

Someone yelled, "That's the Yanks looking for us."

Lester said, "Didn't someone pick up some flares? Whoever that was, for God's sake fire one or two. This is the closest we have come to being rescued in weeks, so don't let them pass us by."

All of a sudden, a half dozen flares went up. The plane came back at tree top level and dropped some paper that read, "I'll send help. Stay where you are. Be prepared to run across that field and board the airplanes."

The pickup went well. When they arrived at the base, everybody ran out to greet them. There was a lot of yelling, "Welcome home!"

General York called for Colonel McCloud to report to his office as soon as he could get cleaned up.

As Colonel McCloud walked through the door, the General said, "Welcome back General McCloud."

"I beg your pardon, Sir, but it's Colonel."

General York said, "Are you telling me I don't know a general when I see one? I've been told that you don't drink but just one isn't going to make an alcoholic out of you. Besides, it's an order. Did I say, 'welcome back'? Now tell me all about what you have been up to since you bailed out of the plane. I know it hasn't been easy. You look good."

McCloud told the story the best he could remember but, some of it was like a dream.

After the story was told and documented, York said, "General to General, I think I'll let you take my job because I'm headed for retirement soon. Before that, I think I'll find me a job in Washington D.C. and rest a little while."

McCloud said, "I'll serve here for a while. Then I'm going back to school to finish my degree in medicine. I'll try to make a doctor out of myself."

As time went by General McCloud finished his schooling and gave up flying.

HITTING CLOSE TO HOME

BEFORE HE LEFT THE SQUADRON, he called Donald Church in and said, "Lieutenant, all the time we spent out there together I never asked you where you were from."

Donald said, "Well, sir, I'm from a little place near a town called Venus."

McCloud thought to himself, "My God, this man is from almost the same location as I am. Now I wonder how much he knows about the person that I used to be. Also, how many people does he know that I once knew."

McCloud just said, "Sounds like a nice place."

Donald said, "My close friends and relatives are planning a big home coming next May, and I'd be honored to have you join us. You will be welcome."

McCloud thought, "This might just be the chance to visit and see what is going on. I can just be a friend of Donald. Maybe no one will figure out who I am."

After he thought about it for a few minutes, he asked, "Donald, are you sure it would be ok if I joined you at your homecoming?"

Donald said, "Of course, and it would please me more than I could ever tell you."

Lester said, "Then count me in, but by that time I'll be back in Canada working as a doctor, I hope. But we'll keep in touch. I'll take the time off and come."

Donald said, "By that time I will probably be out of the Air Force."

Time went by. Lester went to medical school and then to work in a military hospital in Canada. In May of that year, he got a call from Donald.

He said, "I'll meet you in Venus on May tenth."

Lester said, "I'll be there, but in the meantime, I promised my mother and dad I'd have a little get together at our home for all my friends that worked on me in the hospital and the military folks that can make it. But with the war still going on I realize several of them won't be able to come. It's scheduled for April first, and I would be honored if you would join us, that is if you can swing a leave at that time for a couple of days. If you can make it, it will be held at the high school in Shores, Canada."

LESTER GOES HOME

TIME PASSED AND APRIL FIRST ARRIVED. Donald came, several military friends were there and just about all the staff from the hospital. They all had a very good time.

Donald told Lester that his family reunion had been delayed for a year so it would be June second of next year.

Lester said, "That will give me time to work on my doctor's degree.

After Lester got home after bailing out of his plane, he learned that Dr. Holt had passed away. While he was back in school, before the year was out, his mother and dad both had taken sick at different times and passed away. All this happened at a bad time for him.

Since June second was coming up, Lester headed for Tennessee. It felt good to be going back. He hadn't been in Tennessee since he left as a kid. On the way down he had a heap of thinking to do. He wasn't sure just how he would handle the situation. He had the feeling some half-brothers and sisters had been born since he left. He wasn't sure just how he would go over with them, that is if he did in fact decide to let them know who he was. He also knew that some hard feelings would be among them because he didn't let them know that he was alive and well. He couldn't tell them why, simply because they wouldn't understand. At times he thought it best just turn around and go back home, but he wasn't going to leave Donald hanging.

Lester arrived in Venus and looked around for someone he might recognize. He stopped in at the only restaurant in town to ask a few questions about different people. But didn't learn much except where the hotel was. While he was having his supper, Mildred came in and flashed him a big smile, then asked the waitress who was that good looking man over there. the waitress told her that he had just arrived and was asking questions about people she had never heard of. Lester finished his meal, paid his bill, and he left a message for Donald at the hotel.

A couple of hours later Donald knocked on the door of Lester's room saying, "Sorry I'm late Sir."

Lester said, "Call me Lester and we will drop the sirs."

Donald said, "We'll meet at a mansion a few miles out of town. The hostess is a young widow named June Henderson. She owns the boat building company here in town. She is my fourth or fifth cousin. I don't recall ever meeting her. But they say after third cousin they don't really mean much."

Lester said to himself, "My God, Donald just said he was related to June and that makes me related to him, but he doesn't know it. All that time we spent together after we were shot down by the Germans, I had no idea that he and I were related. I guess you could say, 'small world isn't it.'

"That gives me another problem explaining this situation to my dear friend, Donald. He has a high respect for me. Somehow, I've got to come up with a way of telling him and not make it look like I'm some sort of a kinky idiot. He wouldn't expect a man of my stature to have done the things I've done since I ran away from home when I was just a kid in rags. I'll smooth it over with him and keep his respect. I'd have to tell him the whole story and I just can't do that, although, I guess, all the folks who helped me are dead. But all that will remain a secret. I'll come up with some sort of a story and hope it doesn't spoil our relationship. Donald is a fine military officer and a fine person as well. I just can't let him think I'm a dumbbell and I don't want to right out lie to him, so I'll think of something."

Early next morning Lester and Donald met at the restaurant for breakfast. The waitress asked if they were here for the homecoming and added that a heap of folks had come through headed for the mansion.

She said to Lester, "I don't recall seeing you around here before and you sound like you might be from Canada when you speak."

He said, "Yes, I'm from a small town in Canada." Then she said, "I didn't know that June had any relations in Canada, but you learn something new every day, especially when you work in a restaurant."

Lester said, "I'm here as a guest of my friend, Donald."

She said, "Oh, you're a military man?"

Lester said, "Yes."

She said, "Then your breakfast is on the house. I don't charge military folks for food if they are serving our country and helping to keep it safe. I can sure help a little by giving them a free meal."

Lester and Donald both said thanks and left for the homecoming. Several people were already there when Lester and Donald arrived. Donald went and found June.

He said, "I brought a friend. Hope it's not out of order."

June said, "It will be fine. You are both welcome and aren't you Brad Church's son?"

Donald said, "Yes."

June said, "I heard you were a fighter pilot in the Air Force."

He said, "Yes, my friend Lester and I were shot down by the Germans."

June said, "So Lester is also a pilot. He sounds like he might be from Canada."

Donald said, "Yes, he is a general in the Royal Canadian Air Force and, I might add, a fine person to know."

June said, "Well, I can say one thing, he is a nice-looking man, and you say he isn't married."

Donald said, "As far as I know he isn't."

June said, "My sister Mildred will be after him."

Donald said, "Come with me and I'll introduce you to him."

After they were introduced, Lester said, "Pleased to know you and to be here."

June said, "Excuse me, I need to check on the cook, and make sure the food is coming along well. So, make yourself at home."

Lester said to himself, "That's my half-sister and I can't tell her so. What am I to do about this situation?"

Donald realized that something had come over his friend Lester.

He said, "Let's get something to drink." So, they found the drinks, and both got a soda.

Donald asked Lester, "Did you ever drink?"

Lester said, "No."

Donald said, "Me neither."

Lester said, "I grew up wanting to be a pilot. I knew alcohol and flying would never mix."

Then Lester went back to his thinking about what he was going to do. He thought maybe it would be best to just enjoy the party, then go on back to his doctoring, and live a lonely life without any of his family ever knowing that he was still alive. Then his mind went to what June had said to Donald and Donald told him the name was Mildred.

"So that's two of the family. Wonder how many more there are."

June said something about her father being deceased. He was Lester's stepfather. That pleased Lester in one way, but it made him sad in another, but at this time he couldn't say anything, so he just let it ride.

Mildred arrived with Phillip but when she saw Lester, she said, "Excuse me, Phillip, I want to speak to Donald's friend. I believe his name is Lester."

She had already talked to her sister, June, and found out who Donald was.

She said to Lester, "I'm June's sister Mildred. If I'm not mistaken, you sound like you're from Canada."

Lester said, "Yes, I live there. I'm here as Donald Church's guest."

Mildred said, "Oh yes, Donald is, I think, a third or fourth cousin to June and me."

Lester thought to himself, "I may get myself in trouble but I'm going to ask her a question and see what comes of it." He asked, "How many brothers and sisters do you have?"

Mildred said, "There is June, she is the oldest then me. I have two brothers that're younger than me. Then there were two half-brothers that came up missing when they were just kids, and no one has ever heard of them since. That's been several years ago. June and I spent a lot of time searching for them but turned up nothing."

It was all Lester could do to hold up under such statements. he realized that he had caused the family a lot of misery, but, on the other hand, he was tied down, so to speak, and now he was between a rock and a hard place.

He said to himself, "What in the world am I going to do about this? If I tell them, they may order me off the grounds of the homecoming and disown me as a family member."

The other side of him said, "Stand your ground, Lester. You are a prisoner of war hero, a general. What has happened to you? This is kid stuff, and you should be able to handle it."

Then he thought, "Well Dr. Holt is gone, and my parents are as well, and I assume that my cousins who aided me in time of need are also dead. So, I'm in it alone now."

Mildred said, "Well excuse me. I must find my sister June and see if I can help with anything. My two brothers, Joseph and Harm and my mother will be here soon. I want them to meet you. Then you and Donald can tell them about the military. They talk all the time about wanting to enlist in the armed forces so you two can give them some advice."

Mildred found June and said, "Can I help with anything?"

June said, "No. But you can leave that good looking man alone, because he's mine."

The morning passed quickly; the two brothers showed up and Mildred collared them and headed for Lester and Donald.

Lester thought, "My God, I must have looked like them when I ran away from here years ago."

Lester said to them, "Your sister tells me you boys are thinking about the military."

They both said, "Yes."

Lester said, "That's a good thought. It's rough at times. The pay is low when you first go in, but it gets better with promotions. I'd say give it a try."

One of the boys said, "Sister Mildred said you are a general in the Royal Canadian Air Force."

Lester said, "Yes."

The other boy asked, "How do you get to be a general in the military?"

Lester said, "Work hard, and keep your nose clean and stay out of trouble."

The boy said, "I think I could do just that."

Lester said, "I'm sure you can."

June came on the scene and said, "Let's say a prayer and have lunch. Let's let the older folks and our military personnel go first if you will."

Lester's mother came in with another woman Lester guessed to be about his age. It was just about all he could do to hold himself together. At first, he almost didn't recognize his mother. Then he wondered who the other woman was. It dawned on him that she could be the sister that caused him the problem in the first place.

So, if his dad was dead and that was his mother, older sister, June, Mildred, and the two boys, Joseph and Harm then this must be all his family, with the exception of Tom who was missing even before he left home.

The day was coming to an end. June announced that the hotel in town was filled up.

LESTER TELLS DONALD WHO HE IS

SHE SAID, "I HAVE PLENTY OF ROOM HERE. So, my family can spend the night with me, and Lester and Donald, you military men, can also spend the night here."

After all the people left, except June's family and Lester and Donald, they all settled in the parlor for drinks.

Lester said to Donald, "I realized I had told you I didn't drink strong drinks and that is the truth. But in the situation that I'm in at the time I'm in need of a real strong drink maybe two. I've got a heap of explaining to do and some of it is to you, my friend. So, let's find the alcohol and get a large one or two. When I'm through explaining I sincerely hope you understand and will still be my friend. What I'll have to say about what I did as a child just had to be that way and it still is. I can't let real friends down."

Lester took Donald in another room and told him the whole story from when he was twelve years old and running for his life up until now.

He said, "Of course I had help and if I hadn't, I would have died. Although all the people that helped me are dead, I'm still holding to my promise to them. As far as I know I'm the only one living that knows what hell I went through. I will never, never tell on them. God be with all of them. Now that you know who I really am if you think I'm a low life and a liar feel free to say so and if you don't want to be my friend and relative also say so. I'll understand it. I will not like it, but I'll understand. A man or kid as it were, will do a lot of things to save his life when death is after him."

Donald said, "General I don't know of anything that would make me hate you and or have bad thoughts about you.

147

You have proven yourself to me many times as to who you are and what you stand for. That will stand with me forever. It is nice to know that we are related, don't you think?

Lester said, "Please don't think I've turned into a sot, but I need another drink. I've got to explain to whoever asks the question about who helped me with clothes, medical treatment, and food when I left without any of those things. I just can't leave it hanging on that note. Let's go back in the parlor with the family and I'll do my best to clear this thing up for good."

LESTER TELLS HIS FAMILY WHO HE IS

JUNE SAID, "LET'S HEAR A STORY from our special guest, Lester, or should I say, General Lester." She said, "General, if you will, tell us a little bit about the military."

Lester had noticed that no one had introduced him to the woman that had come in with his mother and he wondered why.

He said, "Well, I enlisted in the Royal Canadian Air Force as a young man and as a second Lieutenant. I was a jet fighter pilot for several years, was shot down by the Germans twice, spent time in their prison. I commanded the fighter plane squadron. I came up through the ranks and finally to General.

"I'm also going to medical school. That's about it because if I told you everything that transpired since I left here, we would be here all night.

"Now for the hard part."

He walked over to his mother, looked her in the eye and said, "Mother, I have a confession to make to all my family. So please hear me out. Let me finish before you pass judgment on me. When I'm finished if you want me to leave, I'll do so, and I'll understand. I'm not admitting guilt here, I just want to clear this up. When it happened, I was doing all that I knew to do to try and save my life."

Someone broke out crying.

He said, "Please hear me out."

His mother said, "Oh my God, it's my son and I didn't even recognize him."

He said, "I know that I put all my family through hell, and it hasn't been easy for me either."

Someone piped up and said, "You were a twelve-year boy when you left here. From what I hear you left with nothing

149

except what you had on your back. I was told that was only a long tail shirt. Someone had to help you with clothing, medical treatment, food, and such. Who?"

Lester said, "That was the hold up on letting some of my family know that I was alive. I had an agreement with friends. and I was not going to tell on my friends. I accepted the conditions that were set up for me. I agreed and I don't go back on my word.

"A Canadian couple was kind enough to take me in, give me a new name, a home and education. I will always love the McCloud family who became my family for what they did for me."

June said, "My God when I first saw this guy, I was in love with him, then when he started telling his story I hated him because I knew then who he was, and now I want to hug him and welcome him to his longtime family. We love you, Lester. I think everyone will come to understand and accept you. In my opinion, you are a great man, and I love you as my brother."

Lester said, "Don't get me wrong when I say this, but when I left here, I was running for my life in my shirt tails. No one bothered to help, so I kept on running until I found someone who realized I was in trouble and came to my aid. They will always be in my thoughts as the best friends I ever had."

His mother said, "It's so good to have you here. Now, if we just knew what happened to Tom." Lester said, "No one has offered to introduce me to this lady sitting here with Mother."

His mother said, "I'm sorry Lester, but I really didn't think you would want to know, but since you ask, this is your sister Hester, the person that caused the problem in the first place. I just wasn't sure how to handle all this."

Hester got up and approached Lester, got down on her knees, and said, "Please brother, if you can find it in your heart, please forgive me for doing such a wrong to you. I thought it would be funny to see what Dad would do to you if I told him a big lie about you and let him whip you. But I had no idea that it would go that far and cause that much trouble. After I saw you running away, I realized what a wrong I had done. I tried to tell

Dad, but he was so fired up and mad he just wouldn't listen. I have asked God many times to bring you back to us, so I could tell you how sorry I am and try to get forgiveness from you for such a crime. I just hope you can find it in your heart to forgive me."

Lester said, "I forgive you Hester. I'm so pleased that my family can forgive me for staying away so long. Now I think we should all get together and set up a network to search for our brother Tom.

Lester said, "Family of mine while I was explaining about who I was someone said, 'You were twelve years old seen running with the rags on your back. Who helped you with clothing, food, and medical treatment?' Whoever asked that deserves an answer.

"Yes, I did get help from several people. These were people who knew I needed help. Without that help I would have died. I owe them all my life. I made a promise to them that I would never tell who they were. Although they are all dead by now, I will never tell on them. I hope you can understand my reasoning.

"I would like to say in closing I thank all of you from the bottom of my heart for accepting me as a family member after what I've done to you. I love all of you and I'm so pleased to see and be with my family again. God bless all of you"

As time went on, Lester got to know his family better.

He and his sister June organized the search for Tom.

Lester said, "We'll start at the fishing hole where I last saw Tom. We saw some strangers coming and I had the feeling they were going to hurt us. They had already gotten hold of Tom before I could run home to get help. When Mom and I got back to the fishing hole Tom and the men were gone.

"We went down the river looking for Tom, but they had already gone.

"That's all I know about Tom, and we'll go from there with our search.

OH MY GOODNESS

LESTER WASN'T SURE HE SHOULD GET MARRIED. He just wasn't sure if he could be what a husband should be to a woman. The damage done to his private parts when his stepfather whipped him just never felt right. One of his military doctors told him that there wasn't anything that could be done for him that would guarantee a fix. For one thing it had been let go too long. Even if he had tried to get something done shortly after it happened, more than likely it would have been the same thing. There was just too much damage done. Some of his family asked him why a good-looking man like him never got married. He just said, "I guess I never met the right woman plus I've been a busy man."

He would just let it go at that and hope his answer satisfied them.

However, Lester had just hired a new housekeeper by the name of Sara Linebaugh. She was younger than his other housekeepers had been. One day after Lester had finished with his patients for the day, Lester sat down with Sara.

"I know you wonder why I'm not married. But you've had the good manners not to ask me about that. Well, I'll tell you." He told her what his stepfather had done to him. He finished up by saying, "But if you could put up with that, will you marry me?

Sara laughed, "My husband treated me so badly that I cannot have children. Can you put up with that?"

At that they fell into each other's arms. Not much later, they married. With all of Lester's family and friends and all of Sara's, it was a very large wedding.

A little bit about the author.

THAT'S ME, ARNOLD CROSS. This is my fourth book and my last. I'm eighty- eight years old and I'm not a writer I just enjoy putting a few words together and see how they look.

I spend my time on what I dearly love to do, building mandolins, Cross Mandolins. Each one is a challenge. I love a challenge, plus it's relaxing to me. When I built this house, I planned a full-size basement. That's where my workshop is. It stays in a mess most of the time, but it's mine. When I'm working on a mandolin, sometimes I nod off and dream of when I was a young kid on the farm in the Cumberland mountains of East Tennessee.

A few years ago, I went back to the old farm where I worked the fields with the help of my three younger sisters: Nora, Zora, and Evelyn. At that time there were no giveaway funds from the government. If there were, we didn't get any of it.

We made our living working the farm, while Dad worked in the log woods. Anyway, I wanted to have a look see at the old farm that seemed so big when we worked it. But when I got there and looked it over, it seemed so small.

I parked my truck along the old dirt road, crawled over the old rail fence, and walked over on the hill that overlooked the bottom land. That's where we planted and raised our corn. To my surprise a lot of the old farm had grown up with small bushes.

A cool breeze flowing up from the bottom land and the creek put me in a dream situation. I don't know what I really expected but I guess I was just reaching out for the sounds of yesteryear. The sounds I didn't hear were commands to the team that we used to plow the soil, the sound of singing our songs as we worked, or the rattling of farm tools as we hoed the corn.

Those sounds have long been gone and weren't replaced with the new owner of the old farm. When I came to my senses, I realized that I had grown old with the passing of time. The new owners of the farm have a different way of life than we kids had while we were growing up. We worked for what we had and used. We didn't ask for anything from other sources. What we did and raised on the farm we were proud of it. We didn't ask for anything.

www.ingramcontent.com/pod-product-compliance
Lightning Source LLC
Chambersburg PA
CBHW060228180626
46813CB00007B/2991